THE SWORN

BOOK FOUR OF THE K

Robert Ryan

Cover design by www.damonza.com

ISBN: 9798691744181
(print edition)

Trotting Fox Press

Contents

1. The Death-sleep

Aranloth hung in the abyss. No science had plumbed its depth in the days of the Letharn Empire, nor since. No magic had fathomed all its secrets, either.

He rested uneasily, suspended by the powers that had formed and substanced the universe since time began. This was the greatest magic of his people, and it was built on death.

It was not dark in the abyss. Not everywhere. Little sparks of light shone and flickered. There were millions of them, and though each by itself was but a glimmer, when they came together they shone brighter than the sun.

Aranloth's mind drifted, as it often did in the death-sleep. He was like one of those lights. He was closer to death than to life, and those lights were the spirits of the Letharn people, bound to the world after their passing by the magic of the Letharn wizard-priests.

A sin it was called by some. An exalted magic by others. But good or bad, it had its uses, and Aranloth knew them for he had once been a wizard-priest himself.

It seemed to him though that the years since then were greater than the depth of the abyss, and like it, they had no bottom.

He was tired of those years. They were a weight upon him. Heavy as a mountain they seemed, and the burden of memory, regret and loss crushed him.

No man was meant to live as long as he had done. No mind was capable of enduring so many losses, and it was only by an act of will that he had lived and walked the land he loved despite the pain it caused. He had done so because he was needed. Yet perhaps it was time to die. He was close to it now. Even in the death-sleep, which brought him to the brink and which he had slept so many times before, he had never been so near to letting go and accepting the void.

It beckoned him. It was the balm to his every pain. Not of the body, but of the mind. The death-sleep had healed his physical form, as it always did. In that half-state between life and death the functioning of the body almost ceased, but not quite. Its energy became free to heal, and the magic within him strengthened. Both acted together, and embraced by the old powers of the world in the abyss, quickened inside him.

The death-sleep had another use. It was accomplished in the Tombs of the Letharn, and the ancient magic that protected the dead and the amassed treasures of the Letharn Empire from the ravages of time and the greed of raiders protected him from his enemies, too. Nothing alive entered the tombs, unless the charm was spoken that appeased the Three Sisters, the harakgar. No one knew that charm but himself, and a very few of those he trusted.

But the harakgar were their own danger. Their power was great, and while they protected him they could also kill him in a heartbeat. Drifting in and out of consciousness, he could not utter the protective charm. So it was that the death-sleep not only healed him, but also guarded him against attack. For to them, he seemed dead. Even so, at whiles he sensed their magic probe at him, but they drifted away and continued their eternal vigil.

So it was now that he dreamed, and felt the powers of the cosmos about him, but he also sensed something of events in the world as they unfolded. For so close to death, he saw with the sight of the dead, and even at whiles his spirit drifted into the void and spoke with those who had died.

The future, the past and the present had become one to him, for death was an unraveling of time. He saw Alithoras as though from a great distance.

The marching of the Halathrin he saw on their great exodus into Alithoras. The elù-haraken drifted across his vision in a sprawl of mighty magics and a blaze of swords. The Shadowed Lord himself, the ultimate embodiment of evil in the world, he watched rise to power before falling. Yet he would rise again, and already he stirred.

Then his vision swept away to a time of tumult when fires scorched the earth, and the seas swallowed the land. Mountains fell, toppling like anthills, and new ones rose crowned by vast clouds of turgid ash and lightning.

Faladir he now saw, as it once was. It was not a large city, but its people were strong and Conduil a king out of legend. He was a man fit to rule, for he asked no man to dare what he would not himself, and his retinue loved him like a father and the people of the city spoke his name with pride and joy.

Yet in the slow blink of an eye, Conduil had grown old. Or so it seemed to Aranloth. The strength left his arms. The light of his eyes dimmed. Even his mind lost its edge, but Aranloth had stayed with him until the end. Years it seemed to his friend, but to a lòhren whose memory spanned millennia it was as nothing, and the stabbing pain of his sudden passing was still a shock. And that pain never passed. It eased, but it remained with him down through the weary centuries, as did the deaths of other friends.

Aranloth muttered in his death-sleep, and he sensed the harakgar stir. But once more he slipped into the world of dreams, where thought met magic, possibility was born and all of time revealed.

Asana he now saw, as the child he had been when Aranloth first met and advised him. Frail he was, and scared of being bullied. There was great anger in him also, but matching all this, even surpassing it, was a spirit of nobility and endurance that befitted his lineage. Was he not of the same blood that also gave rise to Brand of the Duthenor?

Quickly Asana had prospered, and Aranloth had intervened to have him taught by the great masters of the Cheng. At first, they had done so grudgingly and only as a favor for what Aranloth had done for them in the past. But that changed swiftly as the boy grew to a man and his rare skills blossomed.

Few there were in his youth who could have stood against him, and he was better now as a swordsman than he was then, for his was a spirit that found harmony in the blade and ever sought to perfect it. He had outstripped all the masters, and his skill was become greater than theirs. There was no one to teach him now, yet still he practiced and increased his skill each day.

But death would steal him away, too. It nearly had. Dimly, Aranloth beheld the scenes of battle in Danath Elbar. Asana had led the defense, and he had not fled to avoid the death he thought was coming. Aranloth was proud of him then, and his friend Kubodin. That little man had more to him than the others guessed.

Kareste also had been brave, and she was burdened with great responsibility. She thought him dead, and she had assumed the task that had been his. Well did he know the weight of that. It was a suffocating feeling, and it would break people of lesser stature than her. But she had endured, and she could fulfil his role into the future. She had the heart.

But it was of Ferla and Faran that he felt most proud. They had learned, and they had endured, and they had shaped themselves into tools that destiny could use. Yet still the chances of the world were against them, for their enemies were strong, and the sorcery that supported the Morleth Knights gave them powers that even lòhrens would fear to face.

Faran and Ferla needed him, and he felt the pull on his spirit to go to their aid. But he was tired, bereft of strength, and he drifted again on the dark currents of the void.

Now he saw, as though from a great distance, the marching of soldiers through the streets of Faladir, and the sound of their passing was as thunder. Homes were charred, and people lay dead and dying in the street. The sky burned red with old smoke, and the air was rank with ash and death.

Through the dark skies, creatures of the old world flew, and at times they dipped down low and were lost to sight. Yet still the screams came to him moments later of some unfortunate soul caught without shelter or unable to defend themselves.

Faladir was become a place of death. It stank of it, and high above in the Tower of the Stone a baleful light shone, casting dark shadows across the city, and beyond. The evil there would not cease. City after city would be turned into this nightmare, realm after realm until all Alithoras was the same.

Aranloth drifted again, and mercifully the scene faded. Yet he wondered if it were a vision of the present or of the future. When all things were one, it was hard to tell. Perhaps it was neither, and merely a warning sent to him by the land itself, for he felt the sorrow of the Lady of the Land all around him.

Mercifully, no new vision came. This was memory, and he saw himself now in the cabin by the lake. The others had escaped through the tunnel, and he had intended to follow. But Lindercroft had pressed home his attack, and the opportunity was lost. Instead, he had collapsed the tunnel, ensuring the others could elude their enemies and he had turned to face them all by himself.

The memory of that was bitter. He was weak from long years of toil, and his last battle with the dark creature that had pursued them to the cabin. But he had fought, and where he could not fight he had used magic to conceal and trick.

The end was the worst though. The cabin had been fired, and Lindercroft waited without. Again he had fought, but wounded by magic and sword he had managed to flee. Yet the enemy pursued him, and well that it was so.

The time Lindercroft spent on that, deeming that if he could kill Aranloth his standing before the king would rise, helped the others escape. And several times Lindercroft had caught up to him, sensing victory. But he knew nothing of the death-sleep, and little about the tombs. The memory of his chagrin as he saw his quarry slip into their protection, and when he realized that it was death to him if he tried to follow, was a picture of mental anguish.

Lindercroft had been foolish, and driven by pride. He sought to enhance his reputation rather than fulfil the task given to him. It had been a mistake, but not his worst.

The knight had underestimated Ferla, and she had used that to her advantage. Their duel Aranloth now saw, and he was proud of her for she had the heart to seize her destiny. He wanted to be with her, for her quest had only begun and she would need help.

But the void called to him. It beckoned like cool water to a thirsty man, or sleep to one who was bone-weary. He was too old, too fatigued in spirit to do what must be done. What he needed was not the death-sleep, but true death. That alone would carry away his burdens. It was time to leave toil, trouble and regret behind. His thought reached out to Kareste. She must assume his responsibilities, and she was a fitting replacement for him. She was greater than she knew.

Once more he drifted on the currents of magic, and in the abyss the harakgar passed him by and gave him no attention.

2. Seeking Destiny

Faran was alone. The others were inside Danath Elbar, but he was outside and would heed Kareste's advice. *Don't wander far*, she had warned.

It was good advice, and he would follow it. He would be a fool not to, yet still he felt a need in him to be by himself and to think.

The top of the mountain was as it always was. There was beauty here, and serenity. But not for him. At least not today. The signs of the battle that had taken place here were nearly gone. All that remained was some trampled grass, and Lindercroft's grave. It was almost like it had never happened.

Yet it had, and the world was now a profoundly changed place.

The wind was light on the mountain top, yet above, the sky was ribboned with thin clouds, stretched by some gale not felt on the earth far below.

He looked to the sky often, and he was glad that it was not overcast. He could see clearly, and there was no sign of elù-draks. It was chiefly of them that he had to be wary, but there was no fog or low cloud in which they could hide. He was safe, at least for the moment.

The edge of the plateau was not that far away. Certainly, he would not go beyond the flat top of the mountain, but he would risk the short walk to where the slope began.

What had happened to the elù-draks, no one knew. They had disappeared, at least for the moment. But this much was certain, at least. The hiding place, like the previous one, where he and Ferla had lived and learned, was compromised. They could not stay here.

How long did they have before more enemies came against them? There was no way to know, but it would be soon. This place was no longer safe, and yet once more they would have to pick up and leave. Where would they go? What would they do?

He found no answers as he moved through the gardens and onto the green grass toward the southern edge of the plateau.

The grass was soft beneath his boots, and it was a fine day. But he was troubled, and not by the things he had been considering, but by something else that he could not quite grasp.

All around him the air was of that peculiar sort, wild and free and nothing at all like the air in a village or even inside Danath Elbar. It spoke of the great wilderness of Alithoras, and lands that he had not seen and paths that he had not trod. But they were there, waiting for him. The world was yet to be explored, and for all that he had learned recently, he suddenly knew that he understood nothing.

The world was vast beyond his comprehension, and it had existed before he was born, before his race was born and before even mankind had first emerged from the great dark to light fires and dwell in the shelter of caves. Who was he to think that he understood something of that?

His story was but a pebble in a great river of time that rolled mighty boulders down from the mountains and broke them to sand on the long journey to the sea. He was nothing compared to that, and he had seen neither mountains nor oceans but only one bend of the river in its winding path of thousands of miles.

But it was *his* bend in the river, his story. And if it seemed vast to him, then so it should. It was all he knew.

At that moment he also understood what was troubling him.

He came to the edge of the plateau. This was a place he often came with Ferla, but he was alone today and it felt different. Everything would feel different from now on.

There was a smooth patch of grass, and here he sat, looking out at the world beyond the mountain. The smudge of Halathar was clear today, and almost he thought he could make out individual trees. That was one place that he would dearly love to explore. So too he would like to test his skill with bow and arrow against the elves who dwelt there. None in Alithoras were finer archers, legend claimed. He believed it, but still he would like to test himself against them. It was not in his nature to accept second place to anyone. Rather, if there was a challenge he would fight for victory. Winning, losing or drawing did not matter so much. It was the fighting that counted.

He yearned to walk the secret ways of the forest he could only see from afar, but he did not think he ever would. He wished he could shrug off responsibility, and dare to follow his heart. He had heard the elves let no one into their realm, but he had also heard stories of exceptions.

Yet he could not shrug off responsibility. It would not be right, and he had promises yet to keep to the innocent dead of his village. He would help Ferla try to bring justice to a realm where dark sorcery and evil had begun to prosper.

But was that his destiny? Was that his sole purpose in life?

It was time to consider what was troubling him most. He knew what it was, now. What would he achieve with his life?

He felt proud of Ferla, and he would do anything for her. But it had been easier when he thought he could do it without becoming a knight. Now, not only would he never be a knight, but he was no longer the focus of attention. Ferla was now the instrument of destiny, and he was only a helper.

He smiled at that. Had she ever thought of herself as *his* helper? If he knew her, and he did, she would have always thought they were in this together.

That was how he would approach it. He cared nothing for fame. All that mattered was overthrowing the king and bringing justice back into the land he loved. They would do it together. Or they would fail together.

How long had she known she was the seventh knight? He smiled at that. He had never guessed it, but the moment she said the words he felt the truth of them. But he did not think destiny, if there was even such a thing, had been determined until she shaped it herself with those words. And more than likely, she had not been sure herself until that very moment. It was the words that created the destiny. It was the choice that made her who she was.

But the long-dead queen of the Letharn had known. He shuddered, thinking back to his time in those dismal tombs. He would never go back, and he wished he could forget them. But not what the queen had said.

The queen had *known*. What was it she had foretold about Ferla? Something along the lines of the quiet one whose name would echo across the land. There had been more, but he had forgotten. Yet that was enough. It could mean many things, but it was clear now that the queen knew Ferla would become the seventh knight.

Her words were vague and hard to remember. It was also said that the dead spoke in riddles. But what had she said about him? If she was right about Ferla, she would be right about him too.

He knew there was more, but he did remember this. It was something about him not being who he thought he was.

That brought a smile to his face. The meaning was clear enough there. He had thought he was the man destined to be the seventh knight, even though he refused that fate. But he was something else.

What else had the queen said about him? Something about a burden he had to carry and it would be heavier than most men's. He wished he had paid more attention. But maybe it wouldn't have helped. That really was a riddle.

Gazing out at the forest far, far below he got the feeling that change was in the air. It was like the world was breathless, waiting. Everything was silent. It was an uneasy feeling, and his instincts quickened to life with the threat of danger and his heart thudded.

Diving and rolling, he drew his sword and came to his feet ready to fight. He wore no armor today, but he went nowhere without the sword and he would sell his life dearly.

It was only Asana though. His teacher had approached silently, as was his wont. He had drawn no weapon, but this was part of his training. Always he pushed his two students to hone their instincts and be wary. You could not fight a man if he stabbed you in the back by stealth.

Asana merely grinned at him, and slowly Faran sheathed the sword, but his heart still thudded. It was just a part of their daily training, but this much was different: Asana had never smiled before. But now his face was lit up and his eyes danced with amusement.

Ever since the battle with Lindercroft, he had been like this. It was as though he was a different man. He smiled and grinned and jested constantly with Kubodin.

But perhaps this was his real self. The man they had known before was one who had believed he was soon to die. That had come out after the battle as well, and Faran was even more in awe of him. He had taught his students despite thinking it would ultimately cause his death.

"Nicely done, Faran." Asana said. His lips still twitched. "I tried hard to sneak up on you then, but perhaps just now isn't a good time for our usual games. We're still on edge."

He said no more, but Faran read in his gaze what he thought. Faran himself was more on edge than anyone else, and he was right

"Shall we sit together a little while?"

They did so and looked out at the vast expanse of Alithoras.

"What troubles you?" Asana asked eventually.

Faran trusted this man, and he knew it would be good to get things off his chest.

"I never wanted to be the seventh knight. And I'm glad it's Ferla instead. Although it puts her at even greater risk, but she's willing to shoulder that responsibility. But I feel lost, myself. Who am I? What is my purpose? Do I even have one?"

Asana nodded. "Troubling thoughts, to be sure." He leaned back, placing his arms behind him. "I once had a friend. He had a favorite saying, which was that it's good to be normal."

Faran looked out at Halathar. "Do you think that's my lot in life then? To be normal?"

Asana laughed. "You could wish it was so. Being something else is dangerous. But in truth, you are anything but normal. My advice though is to wait and see. Ferla has found her destiny. Yours will come too. But don't seek it out. A destiny is a dangerous thing. Let it find you, and enjoy your life as best as circumstances permit until then."

They sounded like wise words. But they also gave the impression that Asana knew something he was not saying.

3. The Mark of Danger

The next day, the little group left the mountain. It was past time that they did so, for danger grew rapidly every day they did not.

Faran thought they had timed it right, though. They had needed a few days to recover from their injuries. It would have done them no good to escape the mountain earlier only to be waylaid in the wild somewhere and unable to fight properly. That was a death sentence.

Kubodin had suffered the worst injuries. But the little man had shrugged them off quickly. He was not as well as he pretended though, yet Faran would still not like to take him on, injured or not. He had proved himself nearly Asana's equal as a warrior, but he also possessed some strange kind of magic.

They were headed down the southern slope of the mountain, the same side Faran and Ferla had first come up what now seemed long ago. But on the brink, they all stood and looked back.

Faran was not sure what the others were thinking. It was probably along the same lines as him though. This was a goodbye. Probably even a final goodbye. The mountain had been home, and it was sad to leave it. There was beauty and peace here. There were memories too. Those at least, would come with them.

He reached out and took Ferla's hand. She squeezed his own firmly. They had both been through this before, but they were still alive and better equipped now to deal with what the future might bring than they ever had before. It did not lessen the sense of loss though.

Kareste was the first to move. Almost, Faran thought, he heard her sigh and then she swung around and began walking down the path, her staff by her side and used now and then as a walking stick.

The others followed. It was a bright day, and warm. Soon Faran felt perspiration bead on his face, but it was certainly easier walking down that it had been walking up.

"Do not let your guard down," Kareste warned them. She did not look back as she spoke.

Faran knew what she meant. He, and the others, scanned the sky regularly for signs of elù-draks, but there were none. They also kept an eye out on the slopes below, and as far as they could see in the distance over the battle plains. Nothing stirred. But that was no guarantee.

Kubodin came up behind them on his mule. He was the rear guard, and also the one best positioned to keep a lookout. It was easier to do this riding than walking down a slope.

The little man whistled softly to himself, and he hummed and even sang at times. But every time Faran glanced back at him, his eyes were sharp and alert. He would miss nothing that was there to be seen.

Night fell not long after. It was a warm evening, and moths filled the air. This was especially the case when they went through some of the small valleys where the great pines grew. It was darker here too, and they slowed as they went, Kareste leading them carefully.

No one said anything, but they all knew if some ambush awaited them it would be sprung in such a place. But just as Kubodin was wary behind them, Kareste almost seemed to scent the air like a wild animal before she proceeded.

It might be, Faran considered, that she used magic to sense what was ahead of her. It was a skill he did not have, nor had it been suggested to him as possible, but he had a feeling that it might be able to be done and even a few ideas on how to attempt it.

They did not speak as they walked now, for they were in the midst of one such valley. Faran moved as silently as he could, drawing on his hunter's skills, and Ferla did likewise. She walked ahead of him, her hand always near her sword hilt, and her head turning regularly from side to side.

They had debated before they left where they would go, and when they would do it. There were reasons not to travel at night, yet Kareste had argued that the dark would hide them, and if it came to a fight then they had all proved themselves. But it would be better to slip away, using what cover was available. On a mountain, this meant traveling at night.

Faran thought she was right, and her view had prevailed. But Asana had not been convinced. Even so, he had deferred to her leadership, and in this he had shown his maturity. As great a swordsman as he was, he had little knowledge of their enemies and the types of creatures that might be sent against them. Nor did he understand magic and sorcery.

But Kareste did, and for all that she took her time and trod warily, she also moved with confidence. They were lucky to have her, and if she was not Aranloth then she was the closest to him they would ever see, and they trusted her.

The stars shimmered in the dark sky, and the half-moon hung heavy, casting long shadows down the mountain. In one of those hidden valleys, where the great pines grew, they rested during the middle reaches of the night.

The grass was wet with dew, but they sat and ate a light meal. When they were done, they talked quietly. All except Kubodin who kept a guard a short distance away so that he could better hear if someone, or something, approached.

"It worries me," Ferla said quietly, "that we have seen no sign of the elù-draks."

Kareste glanced skyward at mention of the word, as they all did.

"I've been wondering, too," the lòhren answered. "It's a mystery, but it can only be to our benefit. I suspect Lindercroft sent them back to serve the king when he was sure we were surrounded and could not escape."

"But why didn't he use them against us in the battle?" Asana asked.

Faran had asked himself the same thing, but he was glad to get Kareste's confirmation.

"The elù-draks are best suited to causing fear from the sky, and finding quarry for their masters. In battle, they can be terrible, for they are hard to kill. But they're not good at fighting as part of a group. They're almost as likely to turn on their own as on us. Nor do they work well together with their own kind."

Faran tried to think what he would do now if he were in the king's position.

"If the elù-draks were sent back to the king before the battle started, do you think Druilgar even knows that Lindercroft is dead?"

"A good question," Asana said.

Kareste nodded. "So it is. But we have no way of knowing for sure. I think it likely, though. Perhaps he didn't discover it straightaway, but we must assume he knows now and is taking steps. The elù-draks were certainly not Lindercroft's only way of reporting to the king."

She did not say *magic*, but Faran thought that was what she meant.

"What steps will he be taking?" Faran asked.

Kareste grinned, but her expression was still grim. Just then she reminded Faran of Kubodin.

"Find us and kill us," she said. "But he'll be all the more worried now. We've eluded his forces again and again, or killed them. And the prophecy will be a weight on his mind. Every day that Ferla lives is a day it will feel heavier to him."

They moved off again into the silent night after that. The moon was lowering, and a bank of clouds rolled in from the east. It grew dark, and there was a sense of brooding in the air.

But they saw nothing out of place, and after the long night ended they reached the bottom of the mountain and walked on the flat plains as the sun rose and the stars faded away.

It warmed quickly again, and the light felt hot when it shone through gaps in the clouds. Kareste, showing no signs of tiredness, found a small gully where an overhanging bank gave them shelter from the sun, and also from prying eyes.

They ate again and rested, and also took turns keeping watch through the day. But there was no sign of another living soul. The mule grazed at whiles, and the sound of it was peaceful. It reminded Faran of the livestock at Dromdruin Village, and he slept well.

When the night came again, they were moving once more. Their luck had been good that no elù-draks had returned, but it could not last. The farther they traveled away from the mountain the safer they would be.

It surprised Faran though that they moved to the south and toward Halathar.

"Are we going to the elves?" he asked.

It was Asana who answered him. "No. But the elves and I have an arrangement. There's a place where

Kubodin or I can leave a message for them if we leave the mountain, as we are, or if there is trouble."

"Or if they ever wanted to kick us out of our home," Kubodin added.

"That they never did," Asana answered, "nor would they. But we were only caretakers there and they knew we would leave eventually. This was arranged to let them know."

"They already know something has happened," Kareste said. "They would have seen the elù-draks likely enough, if from a distance, and maybe even sensed some of the magics unleashed."

"But they will not know that we are leaving, or even if we are alive."

Kareste nodded at that, and some time toward the middle of the night they came to a strange area on the plains. Here, a small collection of trees grew, perhaps some outreach from the great forest that could not be that far away now. But in the center was a kind of glade.

There was something different here. Some sense of magic, and Faran felt that the air was almost alive. Kareste glanced at him, but said nothing.

Aranloth had told him about places like this. There were areas where magic ran strongly in the earth. On such places, rings of standing stones had often been built. Or the people of antiquity had gathered for ceremonies.

But there were no standing stones here. There was a single stone though, half as tall as a man and set deep into the earth. It was white and chalky, and Faran got the sense that once it was much larger, but time and weather had worn away at it.

The stone was of no particular shape, but the top of it was flat, and that appeared to be shaped by tools rather than time.

Asana moved over to the stone, and the others followed. All except Kubodin who held back a little way and kept watch.

"The messages are left with stones," Asana informed them. "Just simple messages, you understand. Nothing too complex."

He reached down and picked up some small stones, only as large as a pigeon egg, from the ground. These were not white, nor was their lying about the accident they seemed. They had been left there deliberately, and they were large enough that neither wind nor rain would dislodge them if left on the table-like top of the larger stone.

Asana carefully laid some stones out in a pattern of three slanted lines. They went from right to left, and each was longer than the previous.

"A drùgluck sign," Kareste whispered.

"Indeed," Asana replied. "It will warn the elves that danger is abroad, and its nature."

Faran was familiar with the mark. Aranloth had told him much about it. It was the mark of evil, and used by elugs and elùgroths as a warning to stay away from a certain place.

"Next," Asana continued, "a stone to represent Nuril Faranar."

For this, he used a stone larger than the others, and he placed it dead in the center of the flat surface. The stone must have been especially picked for just this purpose. It was rounded on the sides but rose to a flat surface where it had been chipped. It looked like a replica of the mountain itself, but no one would be able to guess that or interpret the message. Only Asana telling them that it was so had let them see it.

After that, he placed two stones at the bottom corner of the surface. One was larger than the other, and it was pale while the other was darker.

"Me and Kubodin," he indicated. Then he took a stone and made several scratches radiating out in a circle on the chalky surface.

Faran knew what it was. *Agrak*. It symbolized a group of doves taking flight.

"The rune for flee," he said, and he saw Ferla nodding at his words.

"Exactly so," Asana confirmed. "It's a simple message, but the elves will get the drift of it."

They left then, but even as they did so Asana picked up a rock, the size of his fist, that lay beneath a tree. He moved it to the tree beside it.

Kareste laughed. "You and the Halathrin are certainly careful enough."

Faran did not understand. "What was the purpose of that."

"It's simple enough," Asana replied. "If for some reason the message I left is disturbed, the elves will know at least that one had been left. Shifting that stone was a second message."

"It would also act as a warning," Kareste added. "If the proper message is obliterated, it would mean, almost certainly, that people did it. And that in itself is a signal to take care and be watchful."

They left the little glade then, moving out of the trees and back onto the plain. Nothing had changed, nor was there any sign of the enemy. But Kareste waited patiently for some while, casting her gaze everywhere in search of something out of place before they proceeded.

They only walked another hour or so before finding a hollow in the land, overgrown with a clump of bushes. It was not great cover, and the mule was likely visible, at least from the sky, but it was the best they could find.

There, they ate another cold meal. Kareste would allow no fires, nor did Faran think it would have been wise to do so. A few cold meals were a small sacrifice to hide from the enemy.

"What now?" Kubodin asked. He sat cross-legged on the ground, his axe in his hand and his whetstone rubbing loudly over the already sharp blades.

No one answered. But eventually, Ferla stirred. "I know my duty. I must return to Faladir, and find a way to overthrow the evil that has grown there."

Faran did not hesitate. "I'll go with you."

She smiled at him then, but it was a sad smile. "I don't expect you to, Faran. Likely, I go to my death, and I'll not be responsible for yours as well."

"Nor will you be. You stuck by me all this time, and you could have left. It was your choice. Now, the choice is mine to make, and you bear no responsibility for it. I'm going with you, and that's that."

There was a murmur of approval from the others, and Kareste spoke.

"We have all agreed on this. We are *all* going with you. The evil in Faladir will spread. It threatens all realms and all lands. We will do what we can to help you fulfill the prophecy."

Ferla seemed humbled by those words, and there was a glimmer of tears in her eyes but she made no move to wipe them away.

"Thank you," she said. "I have a task to do, and in truth I'll need your help. But regardless of prophecy, I have no idea how to go about things."

"Prophecy has a habit of being vague like that," Kareste replied, "but the way forward will become clearer as we go, and we can begin to plan as we travel."

Ferla nodded. Then she did something surprising. She drew herself up, and spoke solemnly.

"I may not know yet what to do, or how. But this I swear by all the powers of the universe. I will not rest until the evil is defeated, and freedom restored to Faladir. In pledge to this, I forfeit my life."

Not for the first time, Faran thought she looked like a queen from some old legend, but then his gaze left her and leaped to Kareste.

Kareste struggled to her feet as though something had surprised her. She took a few tottering steps, and her eyes rolled upward before she swayed. Kubodin reached her first, but even he was too late to prevent her falling.

4. A Dilemma of Duty

They all hovered around Kareste, but it was Kubodin who helped her to sit up.

She seemed disorientated at first, but then she gathered her staff and stood again, albeit on shaky legs. It was the first time Faran had ever seen her show any weakness, and he could tell that she hated it. Most people would have remained sitting for a while. But she stood, and she refused to even use the staff as a support, but it was ready to be used if needed.

"What is it, lady?" Asana asked.

She did not answer him, but looked instead at Faran and Ferla.

"I'm sorry," she whispered.

"For what?" Ferla asked.

"I was wrong. Very wrong. A mind just touched mine. It was only brief, and the distance was great. But I know that mind."

Faran looked into her green-brown eyes. They seemed strange to him.

"You have seen a vision," he said. It was less a question than a statement.

"Yes. The mind touched mine, and then I saw what would be if that mind was extinguished into the void."

"Whose mind?" Ferla asked.

Kubodin gently released her, for he still had an arm around her, but it was no longer needed.

Kareste stood taller, but there was a wild mix of sadness and hope in her gaze.

"Aranloth yet lives. I did not think it possible that he escaped Lindercroft, but he has. I'm sorry for the grief I caused you."

Faran stepped back in shock. He could not believe this, and yet it was true that they had seen no body.

"How is it possible?" he asked.

He studied her while she answered. She had apologized for the grief she had caused, but he knew she would not have claimed Aranloth dead unless she was certain that it was so. And her own grief, which she had tried to hide, must have been even deeper than his. She had suffered even more than he and Ferla.

"I don't know. I saw none of the details, yet I saw where he is and how he got there. He was badly injured, both by magic and steel. He *should* have been dead. But somehow he reached safety, and a place that Lindercroft could not follow."

Faran felt a sudden chill. Where could he have gone in such a condition that the knight could not have followed?

"How badly is he injured, and where did he go?" he asked.

He saw Ferla pale, and he knew she had the same suspicions that he had.

"Lindercroft would have followed him anywhere to kill him. Except the one place that would have killed Lindercroft in turn," Kareste said. "He's in the Tombs of the Letharn, but getting there nearly destroyed him."

Ferla spoke softly. "Then we must go and help him."

There was silence for a few moments, but then Kareste shook her head.

"You have a duty to Faladir, and that cannot wait. Things will be moving apace there, for the Morleth Stone is waking and growing stronger the more it's used. You must continue with your plan." Kareste straightened, and she was now fully recovered. "I will go to help Aranloth, but in turn I need the help of one other."

There was silence again, deeper than before.

"I will help you, Kareste," Asana stated. "Aranloth is my friend, and there is nothing I would not do for him."

Kareste gazed at him. "I wish it were that simple, but I may need help from someone who possesses magic. Skill with a blade, no matter how exalted, will not protect against the forces of magic that guard the tombs."

They all looked uncomfortable now, but it was nothing compared to the turmoil that bubbled up inside Faran.

Kubodin stepped forward. "Then take me. I have magic, if magic is needed. But there's not much that my axe can't handle."

"Indeed, not," Kareste answered. "But your magic is of a peculiar kind. It is not that of the lòhrens, and may not suffice in the tombs."

The silence returned again. Faran knew what was needed. He had been to the tombs before, and he had learned the protective charm and the secret of holding the harakgar at bay. But fear stilled his mouth, and he could find no words. Worse still, how could he abandon Ferla?

The silence grew heavy, but Kareste made no move to break it. This would be his choice, and Kareste would not coerce him. If need be, she would go alone to help Aranloth.

Faran felt trapped. He was in an impossible situation. He must abandon either Ferla or Aranloth, but he could do neither.

And yet he must. He thought of asking Ferla to choose for him, but he knew what she would advise. He had to go with Kareste. Nor could he shift responsibility of the choice to her. He must make it himself.

He was surprised, when he spoke at last, how steady his voice was.

"I'll go with you. And I hope," he continued, turning to Ferla, "that you can forgive me."

He saw the pain in her eyes, but he also saw the knowledge there that what he was doing was right, and that she understood.

She moved over to him and hugged him. It felt awkward in their armor, but even so he never felt closer to her than at that moment. It was the knowledge of parting from her that made it so, and he learned a truth from it. People took for granted what they had, and gave it greater value when they lost it.

Kareste looked at him when Ferla let him go. Her eyes were suddenly like Aranloth's. They were deep pools of sympathy.

"I'm sorry. I wish things were otherwise, but wishing is in vain." She turned then to Ferla. "And I'm sorry for what I do to you, as well. I would have been with you every step of the way, and shared every danger. But that cannot now be. Worse, I take Faran from you as well. This much I will say, though. You have learned well, and your heart is one of high courage. If I do not walk with you every step of the way, know that destiny does in my stead. Your enemies fear you now, and well should they."

Ferla hugged the lòhren then, and Kareste seemed surprised.

"It is what it is," Ferla said. "And none of this is your fault. Who knows? Maybe it's all happening for a reason, and will turn out for the best."

Faran wished he could believe that. But a wave of doubt rolled over him. Ferla needed all the help she could get, and while it was her destiny to be the seventh knight, he knew what the prophecy said. She would rise as the seventh knight to challenge evil, but it had never been foretold that she would prevail.

But this much he knew for certain. As soon as possible, he would rejoin her. At least, if he survived another journey through the tombs.

5. The Wisdom of the Dead

The smell of ash was in the air. It was the remnant of fire and destruction, and Savanest loved it.

He had established a camp near the lake. But he liked to wander past the destroyed cabin. Charred beams lay in a tumble of ruins. Most had been burned away, but some remained like skeletal bones. The rest of the hovel was gone.

He liked it here. It reminded him that his enemies were fallible. It was true that they had escaped, but that was Lindercroft's fault rather than any great deed on his opponent's behalf. This was a testament to the fact that they could be located and attacked. The next time, however, they would not escape.

There was something else about the destruction that he liked here. It was symbolic. All Faladir would be destroyed like this, and then rebuilt into a vision of glory. Not so much the buildings, though many of them were markers of the old order, and for that they must go. It was society itself that must be transformed. The old ways of thinking were wrong. A new light must be shone, a new spirit awakened. And destruction was the beginning of that. A field could not be planted to wheat unless it was plowed first.

He would be a part of that. His brother knights too. The king would lead, and with the stone, with Osahka, all things would be possible. Faladir was just a beginning. When it was broken and remade, then other lands would follow. *All* lands would follow. It must be so, for while one land endured in the old ways, injustice prevailed. All must think and breathe and live in the new order.

He kicked at a charred piece of timber, and sent it tumbling back into the ruins. He had come here to think, not to dream of the bright future.

What was his next course of action? It was annoying not to be sure. He had men, but he needed information, and that was harder to come by.

He gazed at the small camp back by the lake. They liked it here, fools that they were. They would learn though. Duty came before swims in the lake and days of ease. As soon as he knew where to go, they would be off and running.

They were fools. But they were useful too. He fingered the were-stone hung around his neck on a chain of fine silver. It was a pearl, or what some called a moon drop. It was nothing in itself, though he supposed it was worth quite some money. But that was not its value.

It was cool to his touch, no matter that it rested against his skin. It was always cool, but at times it seemed to change weight, growing heavier. He supposed that it could not, but with magic, anything was possible.

Osahka had led him to it. Of that, he was sure. Why else had he felt a compulsion to dig into an ancient tomb? It was not even recognizable as such, being nothing more than a mound of earth. But he had felt the need to dig into it, and to discover what was inside.

His men had complained. They thought he was crazy, but their muttering died away when they found the body. Nothing but bones was left, for it was an ancient burial. Neither was there a sword nor spear nor armor. It was no warrior laid to rest here.

Who it was, or what, Savanest did not know. Someone who possessed magic though, that was certain, for around his tumbled vertebrae lay the same ornament that now felt cold to Savanest's own touch. The men had been fearful of it, but he had not.

He had reached into the grave and placed it around his own neck. He knew what it was, and what it did. He was sure the Morleth Stone whispered it in his mind.

So too it had told him to keep digging. And therefore he had ordered the men to do so. Discarding the bones, they dug two feet deeper, and then their shovels struck something hard. A gold box it was, and inside scores of little pearls, replicas of the controlling were-stone that he wore. They too were on silver chains.

The stones he gave to the men. He knew what they would do, but they did not. They thought them rewards for service. The gold box he gave to them too. They could sell it when they returned to Faladir and distribute the wealth among themselves.

Except they would never return. Their fate was sealed now, and their lives belonged to him. He would use them, but how?

He was not sure. He had not known then, and he still did not. He knew now that the transformation the stones engendered would aid him though. But before he pressed too far forward on that, he needed to know where to go.

That was what infuriated him. He knew Lindercroft was dead. He knew their quarry had escaped, yet again. What he did not know was where his quarry had gone.

The king had been furious at that. It was best for Lindercroft that he had died, for surely the king would have condemned him to a worse fate.

How the king knew of Lindercroft's death, he was not sure. Some magic beyond his understanding, no doubt. All had seemed well until then, too, for Lindercroft had sent the elù-draks back to help subdue Faladir where unrest constantly grew. They had taken a message with them as well. The enemy had been found and surrounded. There would be no escape.

Oh, how the king had railed about that. For the next day he knew Lindercroft was dead, but not the enemy.

The king had told him what he knew, which was little enough. He had warned him too that no more failures would be tolerated. Savanest understood that, and he expected nothing less. He must prove himself worthy to be a leader in this bright new world to come.

Yet he remained at a standstill. Worse, he did not know how his brother knight fared. Sofanil searched for their enemy too, but Savanest had been set the task before him. If he were not the one to neutralize the threat of the enemy, he might well be killed. At the very least, he would suffer a fall from grace that would take years to recover from. If ever.

But he did not know where to search, other than southward, toward the hated forest of the elves. The pressure on him was enormous, but he was a knight. Once a Kingshield Knight, and now a Morleth Knight. He would find a way.

Lindercroft had found the enemy. But how? And why had he not given details of where in his message back to the king? That was an unacceptable failure, and yet Savanest understood it. Knowledge was power, and the other knights a threat. The rivalry between them all was enormous, and secrecy was the rule unless dire need intervened. Lindercroft had no desire to see his rivals come in at the last moment and help destroy the enemy. So he had kept his knowledge secret, and taken it to the grave with him.

Savanest felt a chill. An inkling of an idea came to him, and with it hope but also stabbing fear. Lindercroft knew all that was necessary to restart the hunt. But Lindercroft was dead, his knowledge lost to the world…

But was it?

Once the thought entered Savanest's mind, he could not banish it. So what that Lindercroft was dead? He still had the knowledge, and the dead could be summoned.

It would be a great risk. Enormous. Savanest was not quite sure of the rites, but his power was growing day by day. He felt his connection over all the countless leagues to the Morleth Stone, and he knew that would guide him. He had also read ancient texts. Yes, he could summon the spirit of Lindercroft and put it to the question.

This was not a decision to think deeply on. The more he thought, the more fearful and indecisive he would become. The risks were great, but they could not be allowed to stifle the potential gains that were greater still. He must act, and soon. Otherwise dread would paralyze him.

Night was not far away, and already his mind leaped toward what rites were needed. Darkness was a necessity. Midnight would be the time, for in that juncture between night and day where the barriers between worlds was at its weakest it was the best time to act. So too the lake would help. It also was a gateway between worlds, being neither of the land nor the sky.

He breathed in once more the sweet smell of old smoke and ash from the ruined cabin, and then he strode toward the lake. His men looked at him as he approached.

"Wait here," he commanded. "Stay close to the camp, and if you value your lives do not follow me. Move away from here for nothing, no matter what lights you may see in the distance. Or what sounds."

He left them then as dusk fell. He would walk a mile or so away, and then prepare. Midnight was a good while off, but the hours between would be spent in meditation and communion with the stone.

As he walked, the men behind him lit their campfires for the night, but they were small. Already the transformation was beginning, and they did not like the light, but they did not notice. Soon though, they would. He fingered the were-stone as he strode ahead. The men would cause no problems. He must bring his mind to bear on the task at hand.

Night fell around him, sending tendrils of mist from the still-warm water of the lake. Up on the ridges, owls hooted and something splashed in the water nearby. The valley teemed with life, but soon it would open up to the world of death.

He came to a stop at a place where the bank was green with grass and some willows, dark and still in the shadows, overhung the lake edge. He was far enough from the men here that they should see nothing. But that could not be guaranteed. He had never done this before. Yet if they did flee in fear, he could bring them back with the stones.

He sat and waited. The night waited with him, brooding. Low clouds rolled in, and a hint of rain was in the air. The willows creaked, moving to some faint breeze or a change in the temperature of the air.

Savanest thought on his life, and how the world now was different from that of his youth. His dreams were dust, but a new dream had replaced them. One dream, single and overpowering. It was the world to him, and for a while this made him uneasy, but that passed.

He became one with the night. His breathing was slow, his pulse strong and steady. He allowed his magic to rise within him, feeling it stir like a wild animal, unpredictable and dangerous.

The mist from the lake thickened, and he knew it was time. Half the night was gone, and the world now waited for a new day. But for him, it would bring tidings. For his enemies, it would be the first of their last days alive.

He rose smoothly, and stepped to the edge of the water. It seemed black and unmoving, reminding him of the Morleth Stone itself. The magic came to his palms, and without quite knowing why, he placed both hands around the trunk of the closest willow.

Magic flared. Like fire it drove down through the wood. Steam filled the air, swirling with the mist about him, then smoke followed.

His mind chased the magic. Down through the tree he sensed the years, and a history of bright days and winds and storms. Down into the roots, and he felt the thirst for water and the rising of sap. This was the life of a tree, reaching for the sun and delving the earth for nutrients. He snuffed that life out.

With a crack, the tree split in two and fell to the ground, rolling into the water and sending waves crashing beyond sight. Yet his magic flared out of the roots and into the lake itself.

The water near him bubbled and seethed. He withdrew his magic, and sent it arcing as crimson fire into the clouds above. Thunder boomed, and then a single stroke of lightning answered his call and sizzled into the center of the lake. The world flared bright, and the boom of a second peal of thunder rumbled the earth round him.

Savanest staggered, but stayed upright. Then he spoke, channeling his power now into his words.

"I summon thee, Lindercroft. Heed my call."

The waters of the lake roiled.

"I summon thee, Kingshield Knight that was. Hear my beckoning."

The clouds above rolled and shredded.

"I summon thee, Morleth Knight that forever will be! Answer me, Lindercroft. Come!"

And the spirit of the dead knight came. In his armor he rose from the bubbling waters. The wails of the dead in the void rising with him. Water gleamed on his helm. His sword was in his hand, naked steel glimmering with an unearthly light. Blood frothed at his mouth, and gore spilled from a rent in his armor.

Savanest, unwilling, took a step back. A premonition of fear touched him. He had loosed powers upon the world that he did not understand.

The voice of Lindercroft boomed, and it was as loud as the thunder had been.

"Why have you summoned me?"

Savanest felt panic, but he stilled it. "I do what I must. And I have questions that only you can answer."

"I no longer serve, Savanest." The voice of the spirit was quieter now, but there was anger in it.

"You will serve in death as you served in life. The Rite of Summoning ensures it."

The dead man laughed, and it was a bitter sound. "You know nothing, little man. You deem yourself my better, but you will come to heel in the end. But speak. Ask your questions, and I will answer."

Savanest did not like that. Bitter as the dead man was, there seemed still some amusement in his voice. It was said that the dead spoke in riddles, and whatever answers were given must be sifted carefully for truth. But it was also said there was wisdom in them, if interpreted correctly.

"Where did you find the enemy?"

Lindercroft leaned on his sword, and it seemed that the water beneath him grew hard as though it actually supported weight and responded to the will of the once-knight.

"I found them on the crest of a mountain, riding the waves of battles long forgotten."

That answer, at least, was plain enough. Savanest had heard of the mountain close to the elven forest. There, many battles had been fought.

"Where are they now?"

Water spat from the lake, sizzling on the wet bank.

"Where the wind blows and the dead rest unquietly."

Savanest was not sure what that meant. He would think over the words later.

"How did they escape you?"

"They are greater than they seem, and truly among them the seventh knight walks. She is greater than she seems."

Lindercroft said those words with malice in his voice. There was no riddle there, but the surprise shocked Savanest to his core.

"The girl called Ferla is the seventh knight?"

Lindercroft nodded gravely, and the moans of other dead spirits rose from the depths of the lake.

"She it was who slew me, and she is sworn to kill you all. And to bring the king to ruin after."

Savanest could not credit this. She was a girl, and nothing more. Yet the wound in Lindercroft pumped blood, and the waters around him were turning red. Someone had bested him in combat, and while the dead often spoke in riddles they never lied.

"How can I beat them?"

Lindercroft sheathed his sword. There was something of finality in his gesture, and the water beneath him hissed and roiled.

"You may not be able to. She is more skilled than you, and with her are those who are great. But do you *wish* to defeat her?"

Savanest did not understand. Of course he wished to defeat her, but perhaps directly by sword or magic was not the way. He would consider that further.

He made to speak again, but Lindercroft raised his arms and lighting twisted from the sky and blasted him. All about him the water swirled, faster and faster, and a vortex formed. Into this, Lindercroft began to descend and Savanest knew the summoning was over.

He felt weak, and staggering back a blast of cold air tore at him. Cold as the void it was, but Lindercroft's eyes burned with wrath.

"You have answers enough, if you are man enough," the spirit intoned. "But remember the were-stone you possess. It will change your life. It is the means of your success, but a weakness also."

The dark form of the once-knight sank swiftly down into the roiling waters, and the screams of the dead ceased. But a roar replaced it.

A mighty wave formed, rolling across the lake. Weeds and mud crested it, and it seemed to Savanest that a ravening beast, part man and part animal rode its summit.

Savanest fled. He was so cold that his legs barely seemed to move, and fear clutched his throat, but even as the water crashed around him, he came to higher ground and turned to watch it recede reluctantly back into the lake.

A long while he stood there, thinking. The night passed, and the clouds thinned until a faint light showed in the east. His fear soon lessened. He had taken a great risk, but it had been worth it. He knew exactly where the enemy had been, which gave him a starting point even if they would have since fled that place. He had learned more, though.

The girl was the seventh knight. It was a surprise, but even more surprising was that the way to beat her was not to kill her. If not, what was he to do? That was something to ponder, but it could wait. Finding her was the first step, and what would come after could be decided later.

The fear had passed, but he still felt a sense of unease. Lindercroft had warned him. Those words at the end could mean nothing less. Yet there was a promise in them also. At least, if he was interpreting them well. He would change. What could that mean? Dare he hope it signified that in completing this quest and removing the threat against the king and Morleth Stone that he would be exalted above his brother knights? That would be a significant change, and it was one he intended to work toward.

As dawn inched over the land, he turned and walked back to the camp. He realized that he should have asked about Faran. What role in all this would he now play? He was not the seventh knight, but surely he was too deeply involved in the prophecy now to be nothing more than Ferla's companion. There was something else going on there, but what it was only time would reveal.

He reached the camp, and straightaway he sensed the men were uneasy. What they had seen and heard, he was not sure. Something, no doubt. The magics unleashed had been colossal.

At least he knew where to go now, and they would decamp this morning and hasten on their way. Their days of ease and luxury were over. Not that they would complain. He owned them in ways that they did not know.

The master were-stone that he wore, and the companion pieces around their necks, like collars, ensured it was so. Already they would do anything he asked. They thought of him as king, and worshipped him. They would die for him, all fifty of them without question.

He touched his own were-stone, and sent tendrils of magic into it, unlocking its secret powers. From there, he felt it spread to the other stones. He gave the men a sense of ease and trust. All was well. All would continue to be well. There was nothing to fear.

They did not need to know that the magic would alter them. The more he used it, the less human they would become. In the end, they would be mere beasts, dogs that would come to his call. That was the nature of the magic. It was the price of their obedience.

And it occurred to him then that he had a way to track his enemies once he picked up their trail on the mountain.

6. Farewell

The travelers spent the day hidden, as best as the battle plains would allow, and they rested in subdued silence. But they kept a constant watch.

Faran had that responsibility now, on the last shift before they would break camp. Not that he had really rested earlier. He was too upset, and his mind kept racing.

It tore at him that he would be separated from Ferla. From now on, their danger only increased rather than diminished, and though he knew how smart she was, and skilled with a blade and magic, how could he not worry about her?

Yet at the same time, he owed nearly everything to Aranloth. He could not, and would not abandon him. So it was that he spent the day in turmoil, and try as he might he could not find peace within himself. But he knew he must. He was in an impossible situation, and the only way through that was to acknowledge the truth of it and accept the decision circumstances had forced on him.

The afternoon faded toward evening, and the others woke and ate another cold meal.

Ferla approached him, and spoke to him away from the others.

"Why so sad, Faran? We both know you're doing the right thing."

They sat down, looking out at the shadowless plain as the sky dimmed and darkness began to fall.

"I want to be there to help you, but I can't be in two places at once. I'm sorry."

She laughed at him then. "Oh, Faran, I understand that. I want to go with you and help you too. But it just cannot be."

He had not considered that before. But he knew the truth of her words. She feared for his safety as much as he feared for hers. However much he wanted to help her, she wanted to help him.

"It seems," he answered her, "that fate wants us to go our separate ways. But we *will* meet up again. And I'll bring Aranloth with me. All will be well, in the end."

She did not answer that. She knew as well as he did that he could not guarantee it. The opposite was likely true, but she leaned against him as she often did, and they watched the last rays of the sun flicker over the grass, turning it gray and then fading away to night.

They walked back to the center of the camp where the others were ready to go.

"Faran and I know we have to separate," Ferla said to Kareste, "but it need not be for a while yet, I think."

Kareste hesitated, but her head lowered slightly as if in sadness.

"It's best we do so straightaway," the lòhren said softly.

Faran was surprised. "Why?"

"Because we will be followed. The enemy know where we were, so they will seek us there and then try to track us."

"We can throw them off the trail," Ferla answered.

"But it will be easier to do so, will it not, if we go our separate ways and force them to take the time to discover that, wonder what to do about it, and then finally split their resources."

Neither Faran nor Ferla had an answer to that. It was true that it would confuse the enemy and gain more time. And even if they didn't split their resources, it would mean that one group was not pursued. That might be Ferla.

"We can't be sure that they'll ever even find our trail," Ferla said. There was little conviction in her voice though.

Kareste leaned on her staff. "Do you want to take that chance?"

Asana and Kubodin said nothing during this. Whatever view they held, they kept to themselves. Probably, they agreed with Kareste. But they had no wish to cause anyone to be more upset than they were, which was what would happen if the party split now.

But for his part, though Faran did not like it, he agreed with what the lòhren said. But she had more to add.

"There's this to consider as well." Kareste's sharp gaze seemed to take them all in. "The seventh knight *must* reach Faladir. But where Faran and I have to go, to the tombs, will be through the heart of the territory that the enemy will be searching. We will be, at first, at greater risk. There's no need to expose Ferla to this. She can go wider than us, keeping farther away, and swing in around from the west, finally coming into Faladir from the north, a direction that will likely be less guarded by the enemy."

That made up Faran's mind, if it had not already been decided.

"Kareste is right. I don't want to, but it's better to split up now. We'll go direct to the tombs, but you can take the safer route around. You cannot beat the enemy out here. You have to be in Faladir, but first, you must reach the city. No victory is possible without that."

Ferla had reached a decision as well. She liked it no better than he did.

"You're right." She gave a little nod of her head to Kareste as well. "I know you're right, it's just not easy to do."

Kareste seemed to relax. "I know it's not easy. But it *is* for the best, and keep this in mind, as well. Just because we have to part ways now, it doesn't mean we won't join up again later. You know both me and Faran, and Aranloth if he's able, will be with you before the end in Faladir."

"I know, but how will we find each other again?"

Kareste smiled at that. "You are the seventh knight, and I'm a lòhren. Trust me, I'll find you."

Asana spoke for the first time. "I don't doubt you'll find us, but perhaps a meeting place would speed things up?"

Kareste thought a moment about that. "Very well. There is one place I know that will be friendly to you, and they'll help as best they can. Find the Bouncing Stone Inn, near the Tower of the Stone itself. The proprietor is friendly to Aranloth, and perhaps even guesses who he is, although he knows him by the name of Nuatha."

"What's the innkeeper's name?"

"He's called Menendil, and he's a man of judgment and ability. His family have long been associated with lòhrens."

The night darkened about them, and they said their final farewells, hoping it would not be the last. Faran hugged Ferla long and fiercely, then he spoke to Asana and Kubodin, thanking them for their friendship and for their teachings.

"It's a pleasure to teach those who are willing to learn," Asana replied.

Kubodin, surprisingly, put an arm around his shoulder and spoke softly.

"We all go into danger, but we'll help Ferla as best we can. In your place, we'll do all that you would have done. Set your mind at rest."

It was a long speech for Kubodin, and Faran appreciated it. The promises of people were like dust on the wind, but the promises of someone like Kubodin was as iron.

They parted then, and Faran turned as they did so and wished the others good luck. He wished he could have said more.

Ahead of him, Kareste walked into the darkness, and he followed.

7. Who are You?

Ferla felt as though she had lost a part of herself, but she was not going to show it.

Instead, she moved ahead into the night, head high, back straight and stride confident. Even though her heart was breaking.

She loved Faran. She had been in love with him back in Dromdruin Village. Even as she strode ahead, she also walked through the memories of her life, and she found him always there. Everything that had happened recently had only served to strengthen her feelings.

But he did not know that. He did not *need* to know that. It was true enough that he knew her feelings were strong for him, but he thought she looked at him as a brother.

That was not the situation at all, but it was for the best that he thought so, at least for the moment. Their lives were entwined, but both were fraught with danger. It was no time to be sidetracked by feelings and thoughts and secret looks that could distract them from what mattered most just now. And that was staying alive.

For a moment, she allowed herself to think of what their lives would have been like had they remained simple hunters. She would have told him how she felt by now, or rather, she would have allowed him to discover it over time, leading him to it slowly. Perhaps they would already be married, having sworn their marriage oath together under the shade of the big oak tree the villagers used for the purpose in high summer. Perhaps.

But that life was dead.

Now, she had to draw her attention to the task of staying alive. At least, for as long as possible. That may not be long. Certainly, every step toward Faladir was a step toward death. But she had sworn another oath, and if not a marriage pledge, it was just as strong. Faladir needed her, or at least the hope she represented. If, by some strange chance, both she and Faran still lived after their quests, then maybe it would be time to tell him then how she felt.

She was the least suited to her current task, but Asana and Kubodin let her lead. Or maybe they really did defer to her because she was charged by fate to fulfil the task they now set out to achieve.

It occurred to her that it was a test, though. She had been trained, mostly by Asana but also by Kubodin. By coming with her, they were putting their lives in jeopardy. That being the case, they were entitled to put her under pressure. They were entitled to see how she dealt with it and how she led them. If she was not up to that, it was better they found out now rather than later when it was too late for them to leave her.

That was an uncharitable view of things, and they had seen how she performed under pressure when fighting Lindercroft. But still, she would not blame them if it were some kind of test.

It also occurred to her though that it was just a continuation of her training. Fighting a knight was one thing, dangerous as it was, but leadership was something else. All the training in the world could not give experience here. That had to be earned, and it could only be earned by doing.

If she survived, she would reach Faladir. There she must somehow rally the forces of opposition to the king to her banner. That would require not just luck, nor mere destiny, but actual skill. Best that she start that now, even if it was with just two men, and the leadership little more than picking a path ahead through the dark.

They moved across the battle plains. Somewhere only a little way to the east of her, Faran would be looking up at the sky, checking for signs of elù-draks just as she was. But each day they traveled the farther away their paths would diverge.

She saw nothing in the sky to alarm her. Nor did she sense anything ahead. But the greatest danger lay behind them, if their trail had been found. So she paused from time to time and watched what she could of their backtrail.

There was little to see in the dark. But if they were being followed, perhaps they would hear or see some flight of birds disturbed from their roosting place. Or if the enemy were careless, or unaware how close they were, maybe even some hint of a campfire.

There was nothing though, and she was glad of that. So too of the dark. She had no desire to see the bones in the ground on these plains, be they those of the enemy or her ancestors.

The battle plains did not last forever though, and by daylight they should have passed out of the majority of areas where battles had been fought.

But as the dawn approached they came to a vast area of barren earth. In the growing light they could see little grass here. The earth was bare and dry. Dust rose at their footfalls, and there seemed to be something eerie about the place.

"Hey, look over there," Kubodin said. But even the little man, never subdued by anything, spoke in a hushed voice.

Ferla understood why. As they neared, and the daylight increased, she saw the vast skeleton of a massive beast. It was larger by far than anything she had ever seen before, and she wondered that something so huge could ever have trod the earth.

Or flew. Because it must have been a dragon.

The long skeleton was the length of a felled tree. But the rib cage still rose up, each bone, though flattish, still thicker than her arm. The sun had bleached everything to a dull white, even the head that rested on its side a good way off, where the two vast cavities in the bone that once housed its eyes were pools of shadow.

They came to one of the legs, and saw the massive claws at its end, each one that in life could have impaled a man like a spear. Several of these were broken off though at the base, and were nowhere to be seen.

Ferla looked around and understood. She was skilled at reading trails, and this, if thousands of years old, was a trail of sorts.

"They killed it here," she said. "But slowly. See the broken claws? It would have attacked with those, but whoever fought this thing knew how to defend against that. They caught the claws in something and then as the creature moved its own weight snapped them off or pulled them out of the foot."

"I have heard," Asana said, "that the elves used great chains for that exact purpose."

Ferla nodded to herself. She could almost see it, but the warriors who did that were brave men. Many of them would have died.

They came to other bones, and these were scattered well away from the rib cage.

"This is a wing," Ferla said. "Or what's left of it. Again, you can see signs of where the bones have been broken. They disabled its ability to fly, probably with those same chains. But it would take many elves or men working together to do such a thing."

"So the legends say," Asana agreed.

Ferla had heard legends of dragons, but not of how soldiers had killed them in battle. It was a gruesome business, but all war was.

Kubodin stuck his head through the great rib cage and pointed.

"See there? Look at all those arrow heads."

Ferla came closer. She was not going to put her head between the bones like Kubodin. Dead as the dragon was, it was a creature of ultimate evil, and she had no intention of touching it. But she could still see clearly.

Scattered all around were the arrow heads Kubodin had pointed out. They were slender and long, suited to puncturing deep into the hide of a creature. Even so, she doubted most would have had much impact on the dragon. Its skin was supposed to be tough like armor. But she did see that many of the arrow heads were concentrated in the area where the legs and wings joined the body. In those places, the skin might have been weaker, for pliability was needed there to aid movement.

They moved along a little more, in awe of the size of the creature.

"Look at the earth," Ferla said. "See how it's all churned by the dragon's claws in its death throes."

Kubodin stepped into such a tear in the earth and jumped up and down. At the deepest point, normal ground level was up to his calves.

"But how is it after all this time," Asana asked, "that the marks remain? Surely they should have been filled up now by dirt?"

Ferla bent down and ran her hand over the bare dirt. It was hard and shiny in places.

"I think the fire of the dragon was so hot that the soil here has been baked like clay bricks in an oven. That's why nothing grows, and why there's no loose soil to fill in the channels gouged by its claws."

Kubodin took out a dagger and knelt down. Several times he drove the tip into the surface of the land, but it skittered away and on the last attempt he cut himself. He cursed, and wiped blood away from his palm on the nearest rib.

"Well, you were right about that," he said. "The ground is hard as stone."

Ferla did not answer. She was growing increasingly uneasy, but she was not sure why. The dragon had been dead for thousands of years. But she could still sense the residue of magic all about her. Most was from the dragon, but not all. There was sorcery here too, and it was said in the legends that sometimes elùgroths had ridden the great beasts in the air, raining down sorcerous blasts from on high even as the dragon spurted its killing fire.

"Time to be gone," Ferla said. "We cannot spend too much time in the one place, not out in the open like this. We need to find some shelter for a camp."

Asana reluctantly agreed, and she could sense that he wanted to study the scene in more detail. She understood, because it was the nature of a warrior and a soldier to learn how a creature such as this had been fought. Who knew when they would be called upon to fight such a thing themselves? Knowledge was power.

"Let's have a quick look at the head," Asana said, "and then go. I have a theory I want to confirm."

They walked beyond the massive rib cage now, sticking up into the air like bent trees. Ahead, was the long neck. The bones here were still massive, though smaller than many of the others. But the skull was not small.

Whitened by the sun, it lay turned on its side at the end of the neck. A vast eye socket peered up at them, empty and dark. In the long snout, a nostril opened up, and strangely it seemed to Ferla that a wisp of smoke rose from it. She blinked, and it was gone, but her unease grew further.

Asana drew close, and he unsheathed his sword. Using just the tip of the blade, he poked around inside the vast cavity. Then he flicked out what appeared to be a spear head, then several more. He worked at it for a little while, eventually inserting his whole hand, and then he withdrew more spear heads and several arrow heads.

"It's as I believed," he said. "They immobilized it as best they could, and then they killed it via its most vulnerable point." He inserted his sword deep in the eye socket again. "No creature can withstand damage to its head, and they drove spears and loosed arrows into the eyes until some at least reached the brain."

Ferla shuddered. Even in war, that would be a horrible way to die.

"Time to go, then. This place gives me the creeps."

No one argued with her, but even as they began to move away they heard a noise and looked back. The skull appeared to have shifted. Maybe some ancient bit of bone had finally decayed, and Asana's poking around had caused it to shift. Maybe.

But even as Ferla watched, smoke twirled up from the huge nostril, and this time she knew she was not imagining it.

She drew her sword. Beside her Asana did likewise, sinking lower into a fighting stance. Kubodin loosed his axe from its belt loop as well, holding it high with a wild look in his eyes.

"My blood," the little man whispered. "I should have known better."

Ferla watched, and the smoke took a form, hovering above the great skull and looking down on them with disdain.

It was Lindercroft, either in spirit or conjured by the long-dead magic of the dragon woken to life by the touch of fresh blood.

"I see you, seventh knight," the form whispered, and its voice was not Lindercroft's but rather like the distant roar of the ocean.

"I see you, and I know you. For the future and the past are one, and the eyes of the dead see all at once. I see you, and I know your fate. Shall I tell it to you. Do you dare listen?"

"Speak, or speak not. Lindercroft that was, or dragon maybe. I care nothing for the lies of either."

"Brave words," the voice answered. "And maybe wise, or maybe foolish. Who is to tell? Except the dead who know all."

Ferla began to back away. She did not take her eyes from the vision before her, but she spoke to Asana and Kubodin.

"I trust no sorcery. Let us go, but carefully."

They all began to back away, but the voice of the image came at them louder, and it commanded rather than just spoke.

"Stay! You will hear me, will ye or nill ye."

And all three of them ceased to move, such was the authority of the voice.

"I know all and see all," the voice said, and the image ebbed and flowed, moving down from the air above the head of the dragon and standing before them.

Ferla watched, unable to move, and the hair on the back of her neck stood on end.

"You are hunted, and this you know. But he that comes against you is grown greater than any knight. He possesses magic. It will destroy you, or save you. Only I know which."

Ferla found her voice, and though it seemed the hardest thing she had ever done in her life, she spoke.

"You mix truth with lies and lies with truth. You are a dragon, and you are dead. Your power is spent, great as it once was."

The skull of the dragon moved, and there was a rattle of bones. More smoke issued from the nostrils, but the figure of Lindercroft remained still.

"Truth and lies?" it said. "I know truths that would sear your soul and lies that would give you an eternity of bliss. Do you really think you are wise enough to tell which is which before it is too late, or even which is better?"

"Perhaps not. But I'm wise enough to know that one doesn't win a debate with a dragon. It always ends in death."

Lindercroft laughed, and the sound was like the hissing of steam. But out of the corner of her eye she saw Kubodin begin to move, and though she heard nothing, she also saw his lips twitch as though he were chanting.

"Listen to me, girl that was and seventh knight that is. There are worse fates than death. Listen and learn the horror of your—"

But even as the vision spoke, Kubodin broke free of the invisible bonds that held him. His axe was in his hand, burning with fire, and he struck at the image of Lindercroft.

The sorcery flickered, and the smoke that formed it rose, making Lindercroft waver but rise in the air out of Kubodin's reach.

But Ferla was free now too, and she uttered a word of power and with her left arm extended sent a spurt of lòhren-fire hurtling through the air. She almost sent it at Lindercroft, but at the last moment knew where it would best serve.

The lòhren-fire streamed through the air. Blue it was, pale like the sky, but at its edges it burned white. It smashed into the ribcage of the dragon, right at that very spot where Kubodin had touched it with his blood.

She could not produce lòhren-fire as hot as Kareste, or even to the strength of Faran, but Ferla concentrated hard, using the force of her mind. And her magic, if not strong, was not weak either.

White smoke rose from the bones. The image of Lindercroft billowed up in a vast cloud and then dispersed. The dragon lay still, and her fire weakened and flickered out.

Ferla stepped back, wanting to run but not daring to turn her back on the creature. Asana and Kubodin did likewise, until they were a hundred feet or so away. Then they turned and ran.

They ran a good while, for the fear of the dragon was on them. And vast must its power have been in life if its magic still endured after thousands of years of death.

But the fear wore out as the bright sun rose higher, and a new fear replaced it. They were in the open, and visible to their enemies if any were about.

Ferla slowed to a walk. "We need shelter," she said.

No one disagreed. But they still walked for another half mile or so before they found a small patch of trees. They were not of a variety that Ferla knew, but even if they were small they still grew a wide enough canopy to provide shelter from both sun and prying eyes.

They settled down and ate a cold meal. The fear was gone now, and just tiredness remained. But, as ever, they would keep a good watch.

Yet tired as they were, Asana at least still had some questions he wanted answered, and they were not about the dragon.

"It's time," he said, turning to face Kubodin from where he sat. "It's time to tell us who you really are. For you are more than you seem, as is your axe. How do you come to possess magic?"

Ferla suddenly forgot her tiredness. This was something she wanted to know. Twice now Kubodin had displayed magic, but it was not of a kind that she understood.

8. You Are My Family

Kubodin sat in silence a moment. His eyes were dark and impenetrable, his face giving away nothing of what he thought.

"Very well," he said at length. "This is my story, such as it is."

He sat still, only tilting his head as though remembering things long passed.

"You found me, Asana, being tortured by bandits. This we both know, and Ferla has heard that story too. When you intervened, they would not let me go and attacked you. So you slew them. All ten of them, which was no small feat. But hey, you do like to show off."

The little man grinned at that and fingered his brass earring.

"I do *not* show off," Asana muttered.

Ferla knew that was true. But she also knew this was a game between these two.

Kubodin looked away a moment, and then back at Asana. The smile was gone from his face.

"It was a lie. The torturing bit was real, as well you know. You saw what they were doing to me. But they weren't bandits."

Asana did not move. This must have surprised him, but he hid his reaction well.

"If they were not bandits, then who were they?"

"Dogs is what they were," Kubodin replied. And his voice was suddenly fierce. "Dogs on a leash that served another, and did his bidding in all things no matter how foul the deed."

"And who was this man?"

"He was my brother."

At that, there was silence. Ferla could not believe one brother was capable of doing that to another brother, but one glance at Kubodin assured her the little man was telling the truth. His face was hard as a rock, and she knew he was remembering a terrible time in his life and fighting to ensure his emotions did not show on his face. But she sensed them roiling beneath his calm exterior.

"I'm sorry, Kubodin," Asana said. "Small wonder it's not a subject you speak of often."

Kubodin sighed. "No, but perhaps I am wrong to keep it all to myself. I had thought to put my past behind me, and that if I never spoke of it I would forget. But it hasn't been so."

The little man shifted to a more comfortable position, and he did not look at them as he went on with his story.

"I'm the son of a chieftain. A petty chieftain by some standards, but in the hills that are my home on the lands bordering the Cheng, the clans are fierce and wild. They guard well their own, and they're independent. They might be small in number, but they're fierce and strong despite that."

"You represent them well," Asana said.

"Maybe, but despite being fierce, we have a strong sense of loyalty and honor. But we can be ambitious. In some, that trait runs strong. I wasn't the firstborn son, so I wasn't set to inherit rule when my father died. And he was close to death about the time you rescued me."

Kubodin took a sip of water. Ferla had seen him guzzle beer, but he treated the water as a dangerous thing, taking only enough to wet his mouth.

"My older brother was in line to rule, and in truth I had no desire to do so. My life was good, and I had few responsibilities. I practiced with my axe, I ate and drank and … spent time with a number of young ladies."

He looked at Ferla, and she felt herself begin to blush, but she did not look away.

Kubodin laughed, but then he grew very still. "Life was good to me, but by chance I discovered something I was not meant to. My brother was poisoning our father. He could not wait to take the rulership. He wanted it then, and he wanted it badly. I denounced him publicly, but I'm not sure that my father even understood. He was deathly ill, with perhaps only a few days to live."

Asana stirred, but he said nothing. Ferla was sure there was a glint of tears in his eyes though, but he blinked and they were gone.

"My brother denounced me in turn," Kubodin continued. "He accused me of the very crime he had himself committed. And because of his station, he commanded soldiers and I did not. He had me taken captive and thrown in the village prison. It's little more than a pit in the ground with iron bars set in stone to secure the ceiling. Three days I spent in there, with neither food nor water and facing certain death. For I knew the council of elders would side with him. He had cultivated them well, and my father had annoyed them. There was great corruption among them, and they often took bribes to settle disputes. My father had killed several that he was able to prove had done so. But my brother was different. With him, they knew things would return to the way they had been."

Kubodin turned and spat. It was a disgusting habit that he had, but Ferla ignored it. The man was far more than his bad habits suggested.

"Three days I spent in that prison, and I came to rue my inattention to politics. I had time to think too, and I wondered about the death of my younger brother. It had happened during a hunting trip, and somehow he was killed by arrow. It was thought to be an accident, and no one knew who had sent the shaft flying in the pre-dawn dark. But now I can make a guess."

The sun was rising higher outside the shelter of their trees, and it was past time that they rested, but no one was ready for that now. They listened to Kubodin with all their attention.

"I had word on the last night that I would be executed in the morning. I didn't sleep. I couldn't sleep. And that was just as well."

Kubodin looked at Ferla, and to her surprise he winked at her.

"Even though there were a pair of guards set to watch my prison, with a horn to call for aid should anyone attempt to rescue me, a girl I knew, at great risk to herself, had recovered my axe and slipping past them whispered to me and lowered the weapon. I'll be forever in her debt."

Ferla grinned. Kubodin was not like Faran at all, but she could understand why a girl would help him. He was impossible not to like, and no one would ever doubt that he was loyal and would stand by a friend's side until death. For all his imperfections, he was perfect.

"I slept well after that, fearing nothing. For I had my axe, and though weak and tired I could still wield it. When they came for me at dawn, I was ready, and I slew the five men sent for me when they opened the prison. Then I ran, finding a pony and fleeing for my life."

He shuddered then. "That poor pony died a terrible death. For my brother came after me with his men, and it seemed they filled the hills. And they had beasts with them, foul and terrible and summoned from some other place. My brother had a shaman in his retinue, and he it was I believe who supplied the poison to kill my father. And he was rumored to perform terrible rites of sorcery, which I learned was true. One of the beasts killed the pony, but I killed the beast. But now I was not just tired and weak, but badly wounded. I left a trail behind me that I could not hide, and it was of blood."

Kubodin sipped again at the water. "Two days I fled, as best I could, but a group of my brother's men caught me. A pity that my brother was not among them. For if he was, you would have killed him, Asana. Then again, that pleasure may yet be mine, one day, so it is just as well."

The little man ran his hand along the blade of his axe, and Ferla knew that in the future there would be a reckoning between him and his brother.

"Anyway, you know the rest of it. You saved me, Asana, even as I was close to death. They were trying to make my torture last until my brother arrived, but I'm not sure I would have survived that long. And you healed me too after we escaped, and those were dark days and the memory dim because of the fever that gripped me."

Kubodin stood and bowed. "Thank you again, Asana. I'm sorry I hid this from you, but does it make any difference to anything? Anyway, I wanted to forget my past. My father was probably already dead by then. But the truth is, the past can no more be forgotten than the future predicted. From that day onward, there has been nothing but death at home for me, and you have become the only family I have."

Asana sighed. "It makes no difference, my friend."

Kubodin nodded. "Hey! That was a long story," he said. "Now it's time for some sleep."

Saying no more the little man moved away into the trees and lay down to rest.

Ferla looked at Asana, and she was sure there were tears in his eyes now. But he lay down as well and hid his face.

The watch was Ferla's, and she knew she would not have been able to sleep anyway.

The sun rose higher, and she realized that great though her troubles were, they were not the only ones. Evil did not always come from a Morleth Stone. It was in the hearts of men first.

9. Unwitting Fools

Savanest had wasted no time, and he and his men had hastened to the lone mountain known as Nuril Faranar. He did not like that name. He liked nothing about the immortal Halathrin, and Alithoras would have been better if the elves had never come here on their great exodus.

He was not sure that he had always felt that way. His youth was hazy to him these days, his memory not what it was. Oftentimes he reached for thoughts that he knew he had once had, and found new ways of thinking there instead. It was disconcerting, but it was the least of his worries.

Death. Now that was a greater concern, and he contemplated it now. For now he sat, calm and reposed in meditation before a grave. Nor was it just any grave, but the grave of Knight Lindercroft. His sword it was that marked this resting place, and Savanest would know it anywhere. The weapons and armor of the knights were all similar in their making, but never identical.

How many times had he sparred Lindercroft, the knight wielding that same sword? How many times had he spoken to him, noticing how his hand never rested far from it? All the knights were trained to do that. A weapon should always be able to be drawn quickly. But Lindercroft often hooked his thumb in his belt to remind him to keep it close. It was a novice training aid that he had never grown out of.

Nor would he ever. He was dead now, buried in the cold earth on the top of this inhospitable mountain. He would never feel the sun again. He would never walk or talk or enjoy the simple pleasures of a cold drink of water after a hard training session. He was dead, and everything he felt or thought or dreamed was dead with him.

Whatever remained of his spirit was in the void now. Some claimed that in the void the spirit found its true home. Others that there was no such thing as a spirit at all.

Savanest knew better. He had summoned the dead now. He had spoken to Lindercroft across the barrier between worlds. But he remembered that Aranloth had told him once that this was not proof of the existence of a spirit. There were those who believed that a spirit was no more than the shadow of a person's life. Or a reflection of the real thing. But as neither shadow nor reflection was the thing itself, so too a ghost was not the real person. He could not recall Aranloth ever saying what he had believed himself though, which was typical. Always he held back his higher knowledge, if he had any.

The Morleth Stone was better. It was a true Osahka, and a better guide to the mysteries of the cosmos. Not that serving it was easy.

It was depressing to meditate by a grave, and Savanest stood. Earlier, he had sent out scouts to find a trail, but he was not convinced they would find anything. But he had to wait on whatever news they would bring. In the meantime, he must wait, inactive, and that annoyed him.

He decided to walk to the southern side of the plateau. He knew what he would see from there, and he would not like it. But a knight must confront his own emotions and control them. Otherwise, they would control him, and that was a fault of lesser men.

The gardens he passed through meant nothing to him. What use was beauty? It was a construct of emotion only, and it served no practical purpose. A sword though, that was a thing of true beauty. It was designed well. It was efficient. It could kill or protect, and the skill to use it successfully only came after great devotion.

It did not take him long to reach the side of the plateau. The slope tumbled down before him, and he enjoyed the sensation of height. Far away and far below, was the smudge of forest that he knew was Halathar, the forest of the elves.

How he hated them! The elves had thwarted progress long ago. Since then, Alithoras had stultified. It had not moved forward. Things now were as they were then, and they could have been so much better long ago.

But change was coming. He felt it. He lived it. He was an instrument of destiny, and he would help to bring a new order to the world. Everyone would be equal. Everyone would live in prosperity. There would be no conflict to annoy and distract, for those who contested the new order would be destroyed. Utterly.

Several hours passed, and the delay vexed him. But he could do nothing without information, and it took time for the men who had been sent to scour the land to do so and then return.

It vexed him also that he had no elù-draks. Lindercroft had been given full use of them, but he had not. The king had claimed that they were needed in the city. It was certainly true that there were rebels there, but the king had an army and he had only fifty men.

His vexation was forgotten as the captain approached him. The scouts would have returned and reported to him.

"My lord," the captain said, and he saluted crisply.

"What news?"

"The scouts report tracks everywhere. Even down the mountain at many points, and some of these are recent but they cannot tell which was the most recent. They are all at least several days old, even a week or so old. They followed them, as best they could. Some circled back up to here. Others they were not sure. The ground is hard in many places, and a trail hard to follow."

It had been wasted time, but Savanest was not surprised. He had trackers in his group, but they were not highly skilled. The enemy, however, were.

The captain looked fearful to bring bad news. Well should he be, and fear was a good motivator. Yet a man who was always afraid was prone to make errors and then to try to hide them.

"It is not your fault, captain." Savanest told him. "The men are assembled in the gardens?"

"Yes, my lord."

"Then I will go and speak to them. I have a plan, and I *know* they will like it. The enemy are skilled at hiding their trail, and they have a lead in time. But I am skilled also. They will not escape."

He strode back to the center of the plateau, the captain walking respectfully a half step behind him. He knew his place, and Savanest was glad he had not lost his temper and killed him.

They came to the men, and he saw they were nervous, for word must have spread from the scouts. He would do something about that first before he did what he really intended.

"Men!" he called. "You have done well, and I am proud to lead you. Never forget that. It is not your fault that the enemy, just now, eludes us."

He pointed toward the grave of Lindercroft. "It was Knight Lindercroft who failed. Not you. And he has received the profits of his investment. He sowed failure, and he reaped death. That will not happen to you, for I lead you, and I value you, and together we will succeed."

He looked around at the men. The anxiety was dropping away from them. They knew now they would not be blamed for not finding a sure trail to follow. He needed more than that though.

"Lindercroft was tested, and he failed. He was slain by the girl Ferla. He has allowed the reputation of the knights to suffer, and for that I will never forgive him."

He studied the faces before him. They did not know where this was going, and they had never heard a knight criticize another knight before.

"We will all be tested, just as Lindercroft was. It matters not that I am a knight, and you are soldiers. Some of you are young. Some older. Some are skilled with a blade, others have a background as smiths, or farmers, or any number of other things. None of that matters. What matters is this."

He paused. He would let them wait for what came next. Anticipation seasoned a speech like salt gave flavor to meat.

"What matters," he continued, and now he lowered his voice, "is that we are all equal. We all serve the Morleth Stone. But that, my friends, is only a symbol. What the stone will bring is what we *truly* serve."

Some of them knew about the stone. Probably all had heard rumors. Most, likely, did not care so long as they received their monthly pay. But it was time to change that. It was time they knew the purpose they served, and to feel the zeal of that as he did.

"The Morleth Stone is the future. The world it will bring about is different from that in which we live. Rivalry? It will be a thing of the past. All men will be as brothers, and all women as sisters, all working together in unity. Poverty? That too will fade away. The new order will see to it. There will be no rich men, nor poor men. There will only be opportunity to prosper for all, and for all, tasks to do according to their temperament and skill. Our nation will prosper as it never has before."

They did not need to know that some favored few, like himself, would receive a greater bounty from this than they.

"Did I say nation? That is an old way of speaking. Faladir will be no more. Rather, all of Alithoras will become Faladir, and Faladir all Alithoras. There will be no more nations, nor borders nor realms. All will be one. There will be no more wars. One rule will govern all people, and all people will enforce the one law, and that law will be just for all."

He watched them closely now. Some saw the vision of this new world, and he saw the birth of desire in their eyes. Others were uncertain. That was the usual way, but all would believe in the end.

"You are at the forefront of this. You are the pioneers who will go before. You will become a legend, and in the days to come men will speak your name with reverence. But that will come at the cost of sacrifice. Are you men enough to do this? Will you pay with your blood, sweat and tears so that others can reap rewards and your name live in glory after your death?"

Again, the men took this differently, but there was a gleam of zealotry in some eyes, and where it came to the front in some the sparks could be fanned to life in others. This he needed, for what he was about to do would scare them if they were not swayed to his cause first.

He touched the master were-stone that hung around his neck, and it was cold against his fingers. Subtly, he sent his magic into it, and felt it spread out through invisible lines to all the men. They did not know it, but many touched their stones just as he did.

Strangely, he sensed the Morleth Stone from afar. He knew he was connected to it, and loved that connection. But for a moment, he wondered if the stone was doing to him in some way the same thing he was doing to these soldiers. But then the thought was gone, and he knew he must concentrate on the task at hand to bring success.

"Who among you?" he called, and his voice was now loud and full of passion, "will come forward and accept a great task. It will be one of glory, and one that best serves our needs."

There was hesitation, and he felt many pull away in doubt, but that would not last long. Each time he used the stone, his control over them grew greater. What mattered now though was that at least one stepped forward.

More than one did so, though, and he was pleased. Three men stepped forward, offering themselves to his service. They were unaware of what form that service would take, but in the end none of them would care.

He studied them carefully. They were strong men, and warriors. He could almost see the pride in them, the desire to achieve the task he had set, and the unwavering righteousness that he himself felt.

But the gaze of one man was hotter. His eyes burned with passion, and Savanest made his choice.

"You," he said, pointing at the man, "step forward."

The man did so, and his eyes burned even hotter.

"What is your name, soldier?"

"Maldurn," the man answered.

"Are you ready for glory?"

"Yes, my lord!"

"Are you ready to serve our cause?"

"Yes, my lord!"

"Are you ready for your name to live through eternity?"

"Yes, my lord! I live to serve!"

"Then you will be rewarded."

Savanest stepped forward. He did not touch the man, but he stood close to him, and he looked into his eyes. He wanted to study the change.

He sent more magic into the master stone, and he felt it tremble against his chest. It was cold as ice one moment, then hot against his skin like fire. But it would do him no harm.

His power surged through it, joining with it, and activating the ancient magic within. That flared to life, and it roiled uncontrollably before suddenly stabbing like lightning into the soldier's own stone.

The man stiffened, and his eyes sharpened. He did not know what was happening, not yet. But he would.

The change began slowly, but then it hastened. Hair thickened on the man's head, and it lengthened on his arms. It darkened, and grew coarser. His muscles bulged next, and Savanest saw surprise in the man's eyes as he flexed his muscles and felt increased strength.

But he screamed as the magic in him grew and waxed to full strength. His muscles bulged more, and his shirt split and hung in tatters. His eyes held pain and fear, then darkened, and a growl escaped his throat. He collapsed, but he did not fall. Rather, he went down on four legs, for his arms had lengthened, and he was become a beast, half man and half dog.

The change continued. The beast that had once been a man howled, and Savanest still gazed into his eyes. His humanity was gone, but there was still intelligence in the fierce look that gazed back at him.

And, perhaps, hatred. But did a beast feel hatred? No matter if it did, for it must obey regardless. It was now a were-hound, and the were-stone still hung around its neck, nestled tightly into the fur of its upper chest.

The huge dog panted and whined. The men behind it were shocked, but only some in an unpleasant way. The others were wondering how this new development would aid them.

Savanest pulsed magic into their stones. Approval was the thought that went with it, and the men stirred. A moment they hesitated, and then a few cheered in support.

That was only the beginning. Others fell in, raising their voices in wild shouts and cheers. Soon it became a roar, and the sound of it filled the sky and surely the mountain had never heard anything like it.

He that was once Maldurn, yelped and howled, capering around and thrashing his tail. This caused the men to roar louder.

Savanest watched them silently. Unwitting fools that they were, they did not realize that from the moment the were-stones had gone around their own necks the same fate awaited them. They would all turn, in the end.

Savanest raised both hands high, and then lowered them. The roaring slowed and then halted. The men watched him, waiting.

He looked down at the hound before him, and he gave his command.

"Maldurn that was, you will lead the hunt. Find the scent of our enemies. Find the freshest trail, and follow it."

The dog understood him, as he knew it would. Through his own stone he felt a vague sense of its emotions, but greatest of them all was the desire to hunt. The change had made it hungry.

With a leap, the hound set itself in motion, nose to the ground and tracing the many scents that came up from the earth. A good while it did this, crossing to and fro and circling. Then it stood rigid and trembling, before loping toward the southern slope of the mountain.

"Follow!" Savanest commanded, and he and the soldiers followed the hound as it raced ahead.

Through the stone, Savanest knew the were-hound had found what was sought. With his mind, he restrained it at times so it would not get too far ahead of the men.

The chase was begun, and it would end swiftly now. But what to do when he found his enemies? This had puzzled Savanest for a while, but he knew now the answer.

The rest could be killed. But Ferla, the seventh knight, would have a different fate. She would serve the king to replace Lindercroft that she had slain. If the were-stone could change a man into a beast, then the Morleth Stone could transform her from a Kingshield Knight into a Morleth Knight. Of that, he had no doubt.

10. The Magic of the Land

Ferla led Asana and Kubodin, but a fourth traveler came with them. Fear.

They knew it was but a matter of time before the enemy sought them out. Likely, they would find a trail. All this would take time, and should they get enough of a start then they would not be found. Rain and weather would obscure their tracks. Eventually, they would reach lands that were better suited to hiding their passing. A creek that they could cross, or better yet ride a raft down to hide their trail completely, would give them confidence.

But they had none of these things as yet. The plains were not good ground to hide a trail, and they did not know how far away the enemy was and what time they might have to try different tactics.

And the words of the dragon had been disconcerting. It was clear that it was about to give some warning before they broke its magic. But a warning about what? Not that it could be believed. According to legend, most dragons had a heart of evil and joyed in malice and deception. But their wisdom was also deep, and their knowledge of the past and the future far reaching.

So it was that Ferla used all her hunter's skill to try to hide their trail, and even Asana and Kubodin, no strangers at all to travel in the wild, admired her talent.

She found hard ground, where she could, that left little remnant of their passing. When she did so, she changed direction. If there was a cluster of trees, however small, she entered it. Not because it would hide their trail but because anyone who pursued would have to go in there too. That would slow them down, for every time they would have to prepare against the chance of ambush.

The same applied when she entered any of the small gulleys that crisscrossed the plains. They were good places for an ambush, and she deliberately ensured their trail was easy to find here. That would make it appear as though she *wanted* the trail to be found, again triggering an instinct in anyone who pursued that a trap might have been set.

There were animal trails to follow as well. Deer inhabited this region, though their tracks were slightly different from those she was used to. But walking along such a trail helped hide their passage, and being places that deer frequented, it was also possible that they would return afterward and obscure the trail further.

Best of all though was the discovery of a wild herd of cattle.

"Aurochs," Asana had informed her. There had been no herds near Dromdruin, but she had heard tales of them. They were said to be large, far larger than farmed cattle, and looking at the tracks this herd had left behind she believed it.

It was a great stroke of fortune though, for the herd was large, and she followed the passage of their grazing for miles and veered away to follow them where they watered. Only the best of trackers could follow a trail through that, but she broke away from the aurochs on a flat bit of hard ground, and here she even took the time to double back with a fallen branch and remove the slight signs of their passing.

Kubodin said nothing, but he grinned at her. He was less happy at her next trick though, for it required more effort. Not that he was walking. In his case the effort would be his mule's, but he still did not like it.

"We need to split up," she told them. "Only for a little way at a time. But the more we do that, even if we regroup soon after, the more anyone who follows us has to divide their forces and follow all three trails. Or decide at least which of the three trails to follow. Either way, once again it will slow them down."

Several days like this passed. Nuril Faranar was no longer visible, and the grasslands began to change. There were no signs of the battles that had plagued the lands closer to the mountain, and the terrain became more undulating. If they were being followed, they saw no sign of it either in the air or along their backtrail.

They set up camp one morning in one of the largest clusters of trees they had yet found. It was a little forest, perhaps a half mile by a half mile, and in its center was a glade with a hollow full of water. It was little more than a spring, but the water was fresh and clear, and they drank deeply from it before settling down to eat.

When they were done, they talked a little while as they often did and made plans for the next night. Not that it would be much different from the one they had just passed.

Asana stirred and glanced at Kubodin. "I have been thinking," he said.

Kubodin raised an eyebrow, "I hear nobles do that a lot. At least they exercise one part of their body."

He looked embarrassed after saying that, for he had now been revealed as a noble himself, and his old repertoire of jokes would need to be changed.

Asana ignored it, though there was the hint of a smile on his face.

"You are a free man, Kubodin. You have long since paid any debt to me, not that I claimed one in the first place."

"If I'm a free man, then I can keep on doing as I have been doing."

"That's true," Asana replied. "But it's a matter of choice, and you have it. Should you wish, you could return to your homeland and press a claim for leadership of your clan. There must be many now who know what your brother did, and I will aid you, if you wish, against him."

Kubodin was thoughtful. "Maybe it's as you say," he said at length. "Or maybe not. I have a claim for the chieftainship, but my brother isn't the type to relinquish rule easily. Now that he has it, it'll be held in an iron grip and nothing will prise it loose."

"To quote a proverb," Asana said, "when one sword is drawn, a thousand are unsheathed."

Ferla had not heard that saying before, but she understood its meaning readily enough. If Kubodin acted, there would be support for him somewhere in the clan. Those disadvantaged by the corruption of his brother would stand to gain by backing Kubodin. But likewise, those who were advantaged by the corruption would stand with his brother.

"It is something to think about, anyway," Asana continued.

Kubodin grinned. "I'll think on it. I often think on it. Every time you see me sharpening my axe, you can be assured I'm thinking on it." His grin became even fiercer, and Ferla was suddenly glad he was a friend. She would not want him as an enemy.

"Tell us about your magic," she asked suddenly. "You never mentioned that in your story."

The little man lifted up his axe and looked hard at the twin blades.

"My magic is nothing like yours," he said quietly. "It's not spoken of much in my clan, but there are those of us who learned the secrets. I was one. The shaman another. He is greater in lore than I am, but he doesn't have this axe."

Ferla understood. The magic he possessed was one thing, but the magic of the axe was something else.

The little man sat thoughtful for a while. "The magic among my people is different from yours. We are part of the Cheng Empire of old, but there were many, many clans that went into that. Our people are older than the Cheng, and our lore is different. Mind you, theirs is a lot closer to ours than yours. But we are the older people, and we learned the mysteries before the Cheng even thought to move out of their caves and build cities."

Ferla looked at Asana while Kubodin spoke, but she saw no sign of the normal game between them. This was no idle chatter or bantering. Kubodin meant what he said, and there was no sign that Asana disagreed. It reminded her how little she knew of the Cheng Empire.

"This is what we believe," Kubodin said, and he spoke in a reverent tone. "There are spirits who dwell in the sky and land and waters. Gods, you might call them. But we don't think of them so. They are powers, and they have great magic, but they seldom interfere in the affairs of men. Quarrelsome, they call us. A nuisance. But be that as it may, if coaxed in the right ways, through special prayers, they deign to assist us. At least, if it suits them."

It was a concept that Aranloth had once told her and Faran about, but Ferla wished she had been listening more intently. No doubt Faran was. He enjoyed learning this lore more than she did.

"So those times when you have used magic," she asked, "I had thought you were chanting a spell but you were really praying?"

"Exactly. I cast no spells. I just open myself up to the forces of air, land and water. Through me they work their power, if they choose. For that matter, I don't really need to even say the words. They hear me when I think them, and that's enough. But I find saying the words helps me."

Ferla did recall something that Aranloth said. He had not been sure if their magic was as different from lòhrengai as they thought. It might even be the same thing, and who was to say if the gods even existed, or if the invocation of power came from the magician himself?

Kubodin grinned. "Sometimes the gods don't answer at all. They might be busy elsewhere."

That was not so reassuring. Twice now, the little man's magic had proved vital. But it was not the only magic he had at his call.

"And the axe?" she asked.

"Ah, that's a different thing. A long time it's belonged to my people, and to my family especially. It has a bad reputation. Dark deeds have been done with it. Very dark. Then again, in our hills the ways of old still prevail. It's a tough land, and people make hard choices. It might just be that those who carried it were hard men, shaped by their times. Not necessarily bad."

"Such weapons are rumored to influence the minds of men," Asana put in. "We have them too. They are feared, and rightly so. But it is said strong men prevail against them. I have seen no sign that you are swayed by the axe."

"Nor have I," Kubodin agreed. "But sometimes I swear it talks to me, and sometimes I see it in my dreams. But I use it seldom in battle, and it may be that the less I use it the more protection against its influence I have."

Ferla frowned. They spoke of the axe as though it were alive.

"May I touch it, Kubodin?"

The little man looked at her dubiously for a moment, and then handed it over. It was strange that she had never held it before, but as soon as she felt the long handle in her hand, she knew why.

The axe was like no weapon she had seen before. It was lighter than it looked, and the metal of the blades was dark, as though stained with ancient blood. It felt good in her hands, and suddenly she felt a thirst for battle and the joy of slaying. Almost she could see the wild hills that were Kubodin's home, and an endless struggle of clan against clan and raids and fights and the spilling of blood. She had a sense of its history, and she sensed also that there was some restless spirit in the blades. It was more than metal and wood. Discord, Kubodin called it, and that name was apt.

She shuddered, and handed it back. Kubodin took it, and looked at her knowingly. He knew what she had sensed. What powers it had, she could not deduce. But she knew he understood them well. The axe was by his side each and every day.

11. The Old Blood

Menendil sat upon the bench outside the Bouncing Stone, and he soaked up the morning sun. It was close to opening time now, and regardless that he expected few customers today, nothing could dim his good mood. He had soaked up more than just the sun.

It had been over a day since Caludreth had been freed, and much had happened. All morning, he had sat here. And all morning he had received various reports from his lieutenants. One by one they came to him, as though by accident, and they appeared to sit down next to him to pass the time of day before going on their way again.

But his informants had brought him valuable news. It was not all good. Nine men had died to free Caludreth. He had known some of them, but nine was a small number given the task they had attempted. Each death weighed on him, but they had all known going in that some would die. Most had anticipated about thirty deaths, so the result was better than expected. Good planning was the cause of that.

The better news was that no one had been taken prisoner. That had always been a great risk, but the way he had divided the men up into small sections that did not know the whole Hundred would have ensured that not everyone was given up under torture, and tortured they certainly would have been. Better to have died, and he hoped the same for himself if it came to that. He would not fare well in the king's dungeons. Not with his wife being tortured first so that he would reveal what he knew.

But their risk had been worth it. The Hundred had freed Caludreth, and the king had no clue where he was.

It was said the king was furious. He had thrown a tantrum in the throne room, yelling and screaming until foam flew from his mouth. The man had gone mad, which was small wonder. It was said that use of the Morleth Stone did that, but there must also have been a weakness there originally. Otherwise he would not have used the stone in the first place.

But there were ramifications. All night, the Night Fliers, the name many in the city had given to elù-draks, had circled the skies and screamed. No one had gone abroad, and fear ran wild in the city. They made no appearance during the day though.

But terror roamed the streets in daylight too, if not as badly. Soldiers had marched incessantly, striding ahead and thumping their way through the city sending fear before them. That was their purpose. So too the elù-draks. Both were displays intended to cower the populace and show them who was in control.

It worked, at least on the surface. But all the displays of power could not stop word from spreading. Caludreth, one of the old Kingshield Knights, a man admired and respected, a man that was a threat to the king himself, had been rescued from the custody of the king's soldiers. News of that had spread to all quarters of the city, and hope, if hidden, bloomed in every heart.

The king could not stamp that out. Not easily. It would take time. But it was not enough by itself, however good a start it was. What was needed now was to build on that, but Menendil was not sure how. The more he thought about it, the more he drew a blank. But whatever happened next, it laid the foundation for the coming of the seventh knight.

Everything was for the seventh knight. Everything hinged on him. That was the prophesy of old, and Menendil believed it.

He had always believed it. But it had been good to hear Caludreth say it was so, and even better to learn that he had *met* him.

It had happened in Nurthil Wood, apparently. The lòhren Aranloth, and a second lòhren, had brought a young man and a young woman to the forest in search of refuge. Knight Lindercroft had been hunting them. Caludreth had been clear that no precise reason had been given. But he had pieced it together, given news of the fall of the knights at the same time.

Lindercroft had been tracking down the young man specifically, but there was something about the girl as well that drew Caludreth's attention. What it was, he could not say. But he did have the instinct of a knight. At any rate, he was sure that one of them was the seventh knight. Why else would Lindercroft be after them? Why else would no less than two lòhrens be protecting them?

Caludreth had said the young man and woman had come from Dromdruin Village. That was a type of confirmation as well. It was not widely known now, and Caludreth had not mentioned it, but Menendil's own father had been a knight. He had told him once that Dromdruin was the birthplace of many a Kingshield Knight, and that the old blood ran strongly there. The first king's own brother was said to have established a summer manor there and to have lived out his life establishing the province, and many were the heroes out of the Shadowed Wars who served him there. It would not be a surprise at all if that land gave rise to not just a knight, but the seventh knight.

Menendil sighed. It was all guesswork, yet still there had been another type of confirmation. This one had been circulated in the city for quite some time.

Word had spread widely that raiders had infiltrated into the realm and robbed and burned Dromdruin Village, killing everyone there in the process. The king himself had said that to his ministers, and from them that story had gone out among the people. Yet the raiders were never identified, nor a reason given they would attack a simple village with little to no wealth. Now, Menendil knew better. It was an attempt to hide the truth. The king himself had ordered the destruction and murder, and he had done so to try to eliminate the seventh knight. It was typical politics, but that made it no better.

What should be done now though? That was the question Menendil asked of himself, but he found no answer. Caludreth had been rescued. Hope swept through the city, but the Hundred had no plans to utilize that sentiment to advantage. That must change, and soon.

He stood up slowly. He liked it out here in the sun, but it was time to go inside. The inn would open shortly, but before that he would talk to Caludreth. The man was a knight after all, and well versed in politics and strategy. What would his solution to the problem be?

Menendil found him in his room. He seldom left during the day, lest someone recognize him. He had shaved his moustache and cut his hair short so as to lessen the chances of that. And he wore poor quality clothing as well. But the best way to avoid being recognized was not to be seen. Certainly, he never entered the common room downstairs where the patrons drank.

"Have a chair, my friend," the once-knight offered.

Menendil took the one offered, and Caludreth pulled up his own. He sat in the manner of a soldier, the back of the chair before him and his hands resting on its top.

Menendil sat the same way. Old habits died hard, and this was a simple means of placing a protective barrier between yourself and the person you spoke to. Even if it was unnecessary, it was just the way soldiers were. A few years of training became a lifetime's instinct.

"What news?" Caludreth asked.

Menendil told him what he had learned, but did not mention the nine men who had died. That was a burden that Caludreth need not bear for his freedom.

But the man asked anyway, knowing the information was left out.

"How many, friend? How many died to rescue me?"

Menendil told him then, reluctantly.

"It is a hard price to pay, and I am not worthy of it. But still, I have some resources. Later, if I survive, I will see their families paid a compensation."

Menendil was impressed. Nor did he doubt the knight. Until the Kingshield Knights had fallen, no one's word was more highly valued.

"They thought you worth it, my lord, otherwise they would not have made the attempt."

He explained then what his problem was, and how he knew they should take further advantage of the situation and fan the hope to life that had sprung up throughout the city.

"Well now," Caludreth said when he was finished. "The people know that a resistance exists. Moreover, they know that it's effective. That's a good start."

"Maybe so, but surely we can do more. The seventh knight is prophesied, but he cannot do everything by himself. We need to build a foundation for him. Something he can use."

"Quite," Caludreth answered.

The once-knight was silent for a while, and he absently stroked his skin where his moustache used to be. Then his eyes widened slightly.

"The people," he said, "know that a resistance exists. But what they need to *know*, not just *hope* for, is that the seventh knight is coming."

Menendil thought about that, and he nodded slowly. It was true. Knowing something was different than hoping for it. If the people actually knew that the seventh knight was no mere story from the old days, but actually walked the land and would soon come to defy the king himself, then who knew what was possible? Their fear would be transformed to courage.

"That's exactly what we need," he said. "But how can we accomplish it? I can arrange for men to spread the story you told me. How you met the seventh knight and that a day of reckoning is coming."

Caludreth did not answer, but looked out the window in thought.

"Perhaps that's not such a good idea," Menendil said. "No matter how careful the men were, there would always be a chance of their story being tracked back to them. Then the Hundred would be revealed, and many of them taken."

They sat in silence a while, thinking. Then Caludreth rose and walked to the window. It was as close as he could get to going outside, and even here he was careful not to show his face too close to the glass in case he was somehow seen and recognized from the street below.

The once-knight straightened by the window, and for all that he was beaten to within an inch of his life so recently, he was a figure of power now. The king may have stripped him of the title of knight, but he could never take away from him his bearing as a man of wisdom and strength.

Caludreth turned. "I have a plan," he said. "We need something bold. Something striking. Something that sends *just* the message we want, and that the whole city will learn of. But to send a strong message, we must do something very, very dangerous. And it must be in public."

Menendil felt a shiver of fear. But at the same time, he knew he had been right to talk to this man. There was no fear in *him*, no lack of courage. He was a bold leader, but could ordinary men hope to stand beside such as he, and live?

12. For Faladir

During the late reaches of the night, when the starry sky was clear and cold, Ferla called a halt to their march. It was time for a rest, and she chose the crest of a rise to have it.

It was not a hill, for this part of the land was still flat. But it did offer a view, of sorts, and while Asana and Kubodin prepared a small meal she looked back over the lands they had traversed.

There was little to see. Despite the bright starlight, the various folds and rises of the countryside were shadowed. She listened as much as she looked, but there was no sign of the enemy at all.

She should have felt relieved. But she was not. Nor did she know why. But she did have a sense that something was out there. Something.

There was no name for her fear. But that only made it stronger. Was it caused by the words of the dragon? Perhaps. Did the enemy seek her out? No doubt. Did the absence of Faran unsettle her? She knew that it did.

But none of these things were quite the source of her anxiety. Once, she would have dismissed such a thing. But not now. She was older, and she had learned to trust her instinct. Reasoning could only take you so far. Reasoning was what people did when they did not know the answer to something.

But she *knew*. She knew in her bones that she was under threat, and it did not matter that she could not put a name to its origin. It was there. It existed, and she would be ready for it when it came.

Or she would die. But what was it that the dragon warned? *There are worse fates than death.*

"Come, Ferla, eat with us," Asana asked.

Reluctantly, she turned back to the camp.

She ate a light meal, for they were being careful with their supplies. Soon, she would put her bow to use and bring down a deer. Maybe even an aurochs if the opportunity presented itself. But it was better at this stage not to hunt. The farther and the faster they got away from Nuril Faranar the better their chances of never being located. And taking the time, as she did, to try to obscure their trail was already slowing them down.

"We must consider," Asana said, "what you will do when you near Faladir. What will your strategy be? What tactics will you use to fulfill it?"

Ferla suppressed a grin at that. Her relationship with the blade master had changed. She was still very much the student, and getting her to think about these things was just another part of his training. But now he asked questions rather than gave instructions.

"I've been giving it thought," she answered. "But I see no easy way to achieve my goals. I'm one knight against a king, his knights, an army and the Morleth Stone."

Asana pursed his lips. "Perhaps that is the first problem to solve, then?"

"What do you mean?"

"I mean that you must recruit an army. Or cause the people of Faladir to rise in rebellion. Just because you're the seventh knight doesn't mean you're alone. You must become a leader if you are to win. And the people must follow you if they are to throw off the shackles of evil."

What Asana said made sense, and she had considered it before. But her pondering of the idea had never gone beyond the idea itself. She was not sure how to make it actually happen.

"I've heard stories of how armies were raised in the past, but it seems to me that it would nearly be as hard as fighting the king's army single-handedly."

Asana inclined his head sagely. "It must seem that way, but that is not how I advise you to think of it."

"How then would you advise me?"

"Simply this. You are in for a fight, but blades are not the only weapons you have."

"You mean magic?"

"That too," Asana agreed. "But there is a weapon sharper than any blade and more potent than any magic."

Ferla knew what he meant now. "Words?"

"Words indeed. Ideas. And in this case, emotion too. Or if you prefer to wrap it up into one simple word itself, propaganda. It is, I think, what you will need in the days ahead."

It was not something that came naturally to Ferla, but she understood exactly what Asana meant. Words triggered emotion, and emotion could move the world. If she found the right ones, and let them spread before her, she could raise an army ready to strike at her direction. But it seemed still only a little less daunting than taking on the king's army all by herself.

"Propaganda isn't something that we've discussed. It's a strategy of generals rather than the swordsman or swordswoman," Asana said. "I wonder if your training with Aranloth touched on it."

"We did talk about it, and he gave us several examples from history. But it was more in the way of vitalizing an existing army, or demoralizing an enemy force or city. We didn't discuss it in the context of raising an army."

"Nevertheless, what he taught you will be valuable. What was the essence of it?"

Ferla thought back. Her mind went to days in the valley by the lake, and their training sessions there and the conversations afterward when a clean breeze came off the water and cooled them down. Her heart leaped back to those days as well, and suddenly she missed Faran.

"This was the essential training," she told Asana. "Propaganda should never seek to change people's minds. That's a near-impossible task, and the harder you try the more people resist. No. Propaganda should never try to convince anyone of anything. Rather, it should build on what already exists and flare it to life. Emotion is the secret here. Emotion is the language of propaganda, not rational argument. Find a fear, and flare it to life. Find a desire, and make it burn hotter. Invoke that, and people will decide of their own accord to side with you. Men have started revolutions that way, like a single spark that can lead to a mighty forest fire destroying all in its path."

"Very good," Asana replied. "It's no surprise that the lòhrens know such lore. They've long shaped the whole of Alithoras with their quiet counsels. That knowledge is power, so how will you set it to your use in what you must do?"

"That," Ferla said, "I have to think on. But you've set me on the right path. I cannot do this alone. I need to rouse Faladir, indeed, to smithy it like a weapon that I can take to my hand and wield."

It all seemed a cold business to her, and others would die for her ideas. But neither of those things meant it was wrong. Especially given that she was likely to die for the same ideas and with the same people.

"It may be that I'll need to signal my coming to Faladir. That'll give time for emotion to build. When they discover the seventh knight is no mere story, but real, then the fires of rebellion will roar to life. I can use that."

Kubodin spoke on the matter for the first time. "That would be a dangerous game," he said. "It'll help the enemy to find you. It'll make them try all the harder to kill you."

Ferla knew the little man was right, but she shrugged his warning off.

"For myself, I'd rather stay safe. For Faladir, there's no risk I wouldn't take."

13. The Spirit Trail

Savanest and his men followed the were-hound. Often, he had to use the influence of the stone around its neck to hold it back. They struggled to keep up with it. At this, the creature howled in dismay. Savanest knew why. It thirsted for the blood of the quarry it scented.

But that desire was not likely to be fulfilled. More and more, Savanest considered the advantages of capturing Ferla, and taking her back to Faladir as a prisoner. There, she could be induced to serve the Morleth Stone. He did not doubt that, and that would become the final stroke of victory.

If the seventh knight, prophesied in legend, came out in support of the king, then who would be left to fight the new order that was coming? No one.

More and more, Savanest liked this new strategy. He would have to gain approval from the king, but he was sure that would not be an issue. The king was displeased with the way things were going in the city. The more he tried to intimidate the people, the more it seemed they plotted against him. This new plan would solve that problem. The morale of those who rebelled would be dealt a death blow. They would never recover from the seventh knight going over to their opposition.

Through the stone on his own neck, he felt the sudden chagrin of the were-hound. It was in a frenzy, and he was not sure why.

He signaled the men into a run, and he ran himself. It was no easy task in armor, but he was fit and strong. Discomfort and pain were to be endured. Hardship made a knight stronger, and right now he felt as strong as he ever had.

The frenzy of the were-hound grew. Was it under attack? Was the enemy so close?

It was none of those things. Savanest came to where the dog howled. It was a small hollow, clustered with bushes. Here, the enemy had camped. That much Savanest could divine from the creature's thoughts, but little else.

He went over to it, and slowly stroked the fur of its shaggy head.

"Maldurn that was," he whispered. "Calm down. Breathe slowly. Think of what you have found."

The images came to him then. The thrill of the chase, nose to the ground. And then the discovery that the quarry had separated. The hound had followed one trail, then raced back to this hollow and followed the other. The girl had gone one way with two men, and the young man had gone another with a woman.

That woman would be the lòhren, and he sensed her behind this. By all accounts, Faran and Ferla would not have separated. Those two were joined at the hip.

But why? Was it merely to hinder him? That could be.

The dog kept howling, and Savanest casually backhanded it, sending it reeling. At the same time he pulsed searing pain through the stone, and the were-hound whimpered. That too was annoying, but he dared not punish it further. Too much pain could kill, and he needed it alive just now.

This was his fault. He had sent the creature on the scent of the whole party. He had not specified any in particular to follow, but all of them. He should have anticipated that they might split up though.

Did this mean that they knew he was on their trail? Perhaps, but he was not sure how. They must just guess it. But was that the only reason to split up? He did not like not knowing. There might be something else going on, but he had no way of determining how important that was. No, he did not like that at all.

Who to follow though? That was the question. Or should he divide his force and try to follow both groups?

He squatted beneath the shade of a bush and thought. The men did likewise, laying themselves down to rest. Some even prepared to sleep. They were soldiers, and took advantage of a break whenever one was available.

The hound glared at him, its dark eyes glimmering. Savanest paid it no heed.

It was a time to be careful. Lindercroft had made errors, and now his body lay in the earth atop a mountain. Savanest would make no such mistakes. All along, the target had been Faran. That had now changed. Certainly, he must be killed. So too the lòhren with him. She had proved slippery though, as all lòhrens were.

But it was the girl now who mattered most. She was everything, and she was where his future lay. If he captured her, his future was secure. What would it matter then if the others got away?

It would not, he decided. So he would send the hound after the girl. And he would keep his force united. He would need them all, and his own magic, to succeed. Lindercroft had been killed, and he had a greater force. But he had not possessed a were-stone. With that, Savanest knew he could transform his entire company of soldiers. Then, it would not matter how accomplished the girl and her companions were at fighting. Swords and skill were no match against the claws and fangs of were-beasts.

He stood, his decision made, and he was happy with it. Yet it had cost him time, and that was precious. Sofanil was out there somewhere too, seeking the same glory he sought himself. If he found the seventh knight first…

That did not bear thinking about. It must not happen, and speed now was the important thing. He had the girl's trail, and he would follow it relentlessly and drive the men hard. If he wore them into exhaustion, it would not matter. The transformation would revitalize them.

But he must prepare the way. She was dangerous, and their final confrontation would be perilous. She also possessed magic. So, he must hamper her. And he knew how. Fear would drive her to make mistakes and increase her vulnerability. Fear was something he was accomplished with, especially as a weapon, and he knew how to instill it into her.

Smiling to himself, he ordered the men to stay where they were. Not that they were likely to ever follow him.

He walked a little way from the hollow, and sat down cross-legged on a patch of short grass. For what he did now, he needed peace and quiet. He let the tranquility of the plains wash over him, and he put aside thoughts of the battles that had once been fought here.

His breathing slowed and deepened, and he entered a meditative state. For what he did now, he would need magic. The battle magic that he was most familiar with would not serve him. This was a magic of the mind and consciousness. This was spirit walking, and it was something the Morleth Stone had led him to. Aranloth had never taught him such a thing, and probably did not know it.

Anger ruffled his calm, and he pushed thoughts of Aranloth aside. Indeed, he thought of nothing. He was alone in the world, and his body was heavy. Very heavy. So heavy, in fact, that his spirit rose above it, floating upward like an eagle drifting on a column of hot air.

Savanest opened his spirit eyes. It was not daylight anymore. Nor was it night. All about him the world was gray and muted as though twilight had descended. Yet there was no sun. For that matter, there was no moon nor stars either.

He was alone. Nothing living was here. The men were close by, and he sensed them, but it was like they were not quite a part of this new world. They were merely shadows.

All the men he could sense, and he knew which was which. The hound, he could sense also, and even more strongly than the others. His spirit form swept toward them through the air, and the were-hound growled but the others were oblivious to him.

Savanest rejoiced. This was power undreamed of, and he loved to spirit walk. It gave him a sense of freedom. In some ways, his power was greatly lessened. He was no longer a physical presence in the world, and he could not touch or feel anything, but some part of his magic could, if only in a simple way.

But that was all he needed now. He could not follow Ferla, not in the sense that he could in his body. But she was not that far away, and merely by thinking of her the world blurred and darkened. There was a sensation of movement, and when things stilled again he was in a different place.

He could sense her now, his enemy. She was close. Once more he concentrated on her, and again the world darkened as though he closed his eyes.

This time, when the sense of movement passed, he floated in the air and Ferla was nearby. So too her two companions. They were oblivious to him, and he knew that his spirit form was invisible.

That needed to change. He must take form here, for without form he could not speak to her, and that was what he most desired.

He reached out with his thought, and his magic was one with it. His powers were limited, yet still he could summon a mist, and this he did. It gathered around him, thickening, and it took his shape.

He appeared before them in a small wood. They drew their swords, and one, seemingly a scruffy vagabond, held an axe. But there was shock on their faces, and Savanest liked that.

"Are you ready to meet your fate, Ferla that was and knight that you have become?"

His voice was like the sighing of the wind in the treetops. It was mournful and eerie, and he liked it. Here, he had an opportunity to scare her, but also to gauge her character and powers, if she truly had any.

"Begone, apparition. You are nothing here," she said. As if in proof of her words, she sheathed her sword. She was not going to show fear.

"Nothing?" he answered. It was time to disabuse her of her misconception.

Raising his arms, he summoned a mist from the ground, and he made it cold so that a frost formed on the earth.

"Nothing?" he repeated. "You are too sure of yourself, girl."

Even as he spoke he sent tendrils of the mist swirling and leaping. Let her see what it was like to be bound by magic, to be thrown to the ground and to have the spirit-mist constrict her throat.

To his surprise, she uttered one of the great words of power and summoned fire. It swept forward and crashed into the mist, sending it hissing into oblivion. The frost on the ground melted, and he felt humbled.

Worse, she laughed at him. And that he could not bear. Even as Lindercroft had underestimated her, so had he. How was it possible that Aranloth had trained her in such arts in so short a time?

But in truth, she had the advantage here. She was in the flesh, and he was but a thing of spirit. She had her full powers, and he only a shadow of what was his. But for what she had done, he would make her pay, and that would be in the flesh, too.

"Which knight are you?" the girl asked. "Tell me, so I shall know your name when we meet in person, and so I can mark it on your grave."

He felt a chill, but then he understood that she was attempting to do to him exactly what he intended for her; instill fear into the opponent to unduly hasten their plans and put their minds in disorder. He laughed.

"I am Savanest, Morleth Knight and servant of the Great Cause. That will mark my grave, but you and your friends and all you know will be dust on the wind ere that day comes, if ever it does. I will—"

To his dismay she raised her hand and sent a sheet of flame rippling through the air. Almost he felt the burning of it, but he was only spirit and she could only surprise rather than harm him.

Yet still, the fire tore through the mist that formed his shape, and it fell to tatters. He could have reformed it, but he knew she would dispel him again.

Burning with a white-hot rage, he thought of his body back at the hollow, and even as he did so he felt the bindings of his flesh and his eyes flicked open.

He wanted to yell and shout, but he calmed himself. He was a knight, and he had achieved his purpose. Despite her actions, the girl had been scared. That much he could tell, and it was good to know. She felt fear, but she did not let it crush her. That was very good to know, because victory in battle came from understanding your enemy.

And if she was his enemy before, she was doubly so now.

His anger cooled. It would wait for fulfillment, and his revenge on her would be sweeter when it came. Beyond doubt, he would not kill her. Better by far to bring her in shame to the king, and by the power of the Morleth Stone make her serve. Yet some part of her mind would know what she once was, and that she had become a slave to what she hated. That would be the best revenge of all, and something that acted as both punishment to her but also furthered the cause he served. That was perfection.

He sat where he was, and thought. It was time to let revenge go. That, he could enjoy later at leisure. What he must do now was consider what he had learned.

It was small wonder that Lindercroft had underestimated her. She had power far greater than she should have for her age and experience. But her magic was not great in itself. At best, she was only a good student. His was greater.

Her skill with a sword was another matter. He could not gauge that without touching blades with her, but he did know she had killed Lindercroft in combat rather than by magic. That bespoke of high skill indeed. But he would not be fighting her. He would use were-beasts to bring her down and capture her.

He turned his mind to the half-breed that was with her. He must have been part Cheng, and it showed. He was nothing, and yet the steady gaze of his eyes that showed no surprise or fear had been disconcerting. He was more than he seemed, and someone to watch.

It was the little man with the axe that was the greatest mystery of all though. About him, there was little to see and yet much to feel. He possessed magic, and he wielded a strange axe that made Savanest feel uneasy. There was something of magic about it too. But both magics were outside his experience.

At any rate, his decision was made. Both men must be treated as dangerous, and both must be killed swiftly. Then the girl would be his.

He stood and returned to the hollow. Already, plans were swirling through his mind.

14. Hunted

Ferla did not show what she was feeling. Fear coursed through her, but as she had been taught to do she accepted it, and did not let it hinder her actions.

It was daytime, and they had been resting, but there would be no more sleeping now.

"So," Asana said. "That was the enemy. He seemed somewhat grander than Lindercroft. But I suspect he is no better at fighting."

Ferla knew what Asana was trying to do. He was reminding her that she had defeated a knight like this before, and while there was reason to be cautious she had no need for undue fear. She understood what he was doing, and her heart surged with affection for him.

"Hey!" Kubodin said. "You think he was grand? Maybe he was. Just like a rat with a gold tooth thinks he's something special."

Ferla could not help but grin at that. She knew what Kubodin was doing, too. Humor was the warrior's age-old way of shrugging off fear.

She was lucky to have these two with her. Very lucky, indeed. But she was still in charge, and the responsibility for what came next rested on her. They showed no sign of taking that burden from her, and she understood now that it was not a test but a way of preparing her for the harder times ahead.

"We have to leave," she said. "And fast. We don't know how far away he is, but he has to be close to find me by magic like that. We'll have to risk traveling by day, at least for the moment. There's more cover in the terrain now than there was earlier. If we see something, we have a chance of hiding that we didn't have before."

"Do you think he knows where we are?" Asana asked.

Kubodin answered that before she did, and Ferla was surprised even if she did not disagree.

"I don't think he does," the little man stated confidently. "If he did, he wouldn't have given us warning like that. He would have tried to surprise us. Besides, that mist thing was only a small magic. Finding someone by magic is not the same as locating them. It's like a mule finding his way home by himself. He can do it, but if you ask him how he can't tell you."

Asana raised an eyebrow at that, but said nothing.

"Kubodin is right," Ferla agreed. "He did what lòhrens call spirit walking. Finding someone like that is like tracking down a campfire in pitch dark by the smell of smoke. You can do it, but you couldn't describe to someone else exactly where you found it. But he does have a general idea, and the faster we're gone from here the better. Also, I don't think he has the power to spirit walk great distances. He must be close."

"He shouldn't be," Kubodin said. "All your tricks must have led him on a merry dance. But still, I don't think you're wrong. He's not that far away."

There was no more discussion after that. They had not rested fully after the previous night's march, but they broke camp and left swiftly.

They moved ahead just as they had always done. Ferla led, Asana was in the middle and Kubodin rode his mule at the rear. All of them, however, kept a close watch around them.

There was nothing to see, but that made Ferla feel no better. She was being hunted again, and she was beginning to hate that with a passion. Nor did she know if elù-draks were abroad. Not knowing if an attack would come by air or land was disconcerting. But it did not change her decision to travel by daylight, and the others had not disagreed with her.

They traveled at speed. Ferla made no attempt to hide their trail, though she wanted to. What was needed now though was to put as much distance as possible between where they had last been and wherever they went next.

In truth, she did not think that Savanest knew exactly where they were. But when he found the place where he had come across them while he spirit walked, he would recognize it. And he would know exactly when they had left there, and how far away he was from them.

No doubt, he would follow their trail from that place. She expected that, but there was a time to hide a trail and a time not to worry about it. Speed was not the only factor. The ground was even more important. When she came to a place where she could pull one of her tricks, that was the most effective way of trying to slip the hunt. Trying to deceive a tracker over unfavorable ground was just a waste of time.

They rested fairly often, pacing themselves. But they moved quickly when they were up and about, which was most of the time. Night settled in, and they kept going because her regular breaks ensured they were not too tired.

The stars sprang to life above. The smell of dew on the grass, and herbs, bruised beneath their boots, filled the air with a sweet scent. Bats whirred through the shadows, seeking insects, and high above some flying night bird cried loudly. It was not a call that she knew, but it was the sound of wild lands and she was at home.

Savanest was no doubt a city man. This was *her* world, and she was at home in it in a way that he never would be. He must have a good tracker with him, better than she had expected, but that was nothing to fear. She and her companions were strong. They could walk through the night and probably would. When the time came, she would disappear into the wild and leave the enemy dumbfounded.

So she hoped. But doubt nagged at her. Always, the enemy seemed to find her and Faran.

She wondered how Faran and Kareste were progressing. It seemed that the enemy had come after her, and she was glad of that. It meant Faran was safer. Even if Savanest had split his forces, he himself had come after her, and he was the greatest threat.

They walked through the night, and Kubodin often walked too, holding the reins of the mule and leading it forward. He offered them all turns to ride, but they refused. The mule needed to be spared as much as they spared themselves, and if the worst came about then Kubodin at least could escape on the mule and seek Faran out.

The gray light of dawn saw them enter a new kind of country. It was less flat than it had been, and the ground turned rocky in places, which was exactly what Ferla wanted. Now, it was time to confuse the enemy.

They did not stop just because the sun rose. Prevention was better than cure, and Ferla intended to both outsmart and outdistance the enemy.

They came to a rocky slope, bare of grass. This Ferla ascended, and she made no attempt to hide their trail, but coming down the other side she veered to the west and there entered a dry wash bare of dirt and grass. It was mostly just sandstone, and it stretched ahead for a long way, but she did not follow it.

She led them off that path, and back uphill along a patch of short grass. Here, they left little trail, and she slowed down to a very slow walk indeed, being careful to leave as little sign as possible of their passage. When they had reached the rocky slope again, she found a few dead branches from bushes and went back to brush away what little sign they had left on the grass.

"Let them find us now," she muttered.

Kubodin grinned at her, but Asana said nothing.

They backtracked then, coming around the side of the hill and crossing the obvious trail they had left while ascending. But this time they took great care to hide their passage.

They headed east then for several miles, and Ferla was sure that trick would lose them. With luck, they might spend a day or two trying to pick them up again, if they ever did.

The sun was moving toward noon before they took a long rest. Ferla was confident, but she still would have preferred to push on. But they had not slept for a long while, and they needed rest.

It was not a long break though. They took turns to keep watch, but they slept only until mid-afternoon. Then they began their trek again.

Once more they swung to the north, and the afternoon became hot as they traveled before a breeze sprang up at their backs. The longer grass here bent before it, flowing like the sea, and they crested a long slope bare of trees.

At its top, they found something that unnerved them. It was a campfire. Ferla felt the ashes, and they were cold. It was several days old, but then they discovered others. A company of men had camped here, and given the disciplined nature of the campsite, and the evenly spaced fires, Ferla surmised soldiers were responsible.

"Savanest camped here," she said.

"Maybe," Asana replied. "But there might be others looking for us too."

It was a disconcerting idea.

She turned and looked at their backtrail. It was more habit than anything else, but to her shock there were signs of movement far away and she caught the glint of metal in several places.

"How can they possibly have found us so quickly?" she muttered, and a wave of despair washed over her.

15. Trapped and Bound

They fled. Ferla led them at a rapid pace, and she knew it was pointless to try to hide their trail further. All her tricks had come to nothing.

She did not understand why though, and that disturbed her.

The long shadows of dusk seemed to creep after them, and night, when it fell, felt like it had eyes. Where could they go? What place would offer safety? The dark was always a friend to evil.

Ferla chided herself. Her thoughts were superstitious nonsense. She was a hunter, and the wild lands, during the day or at night, were her home.

Fear was beginning to make her think differently, and no doubt that had been Savanest's intention when he had appeared. The remedy to this was information. She needed to know how they kept finding her in order to plan a way to overcome it. But how could she obtain that knowledge?

Far away in the east, a storm brewed. The night sky was dark there, but stabs of lightning could be seen. She heard no thunder though, and the storm seemed to be tracking northward rather than toward them.

She cursed her luck. The storm, if it enveloped them here, would have been to their favor. Wind and rain would have hidden their trail.

Toward midnight, they came to a cluster of trees, and there they threw themselves down and rested. Even the distant lightning faded, and the world was quiet and peaceful around them. But Ferla knew it would not last.

"We need to know what Savanest is doing," she said.

Kubodin eyed her. He guessed what she intended, but Asana did not.

"It's too dangerous to go scouting," Asana said. "Best to leave them be, and save our energy for escaping, don't you think?"

Ferla summoned up a grin. "You're right. Best to stay here."

Kubodin shook his head. "That doesn't mean she won't be scouting, master. But it's dangerous, what she intends."

Asana looked confused, so Ferla explained to him exactly what she intended.

"It was Savanest that gave me the idea. He used spirit walking to enter our camp and observe us. Just maybe, I can use the same trick on him. I need to try, at least. I need to discover how he keeps tracking us. Maybe he's somehow using magic. Whatever it is, I have to discover it before I can defeat it."

Asana looked doubtful. He was of a kind that placed his faith in his skill with a sword rather than magic. But that did not mean he underestimated its uses.

"Have you done this spirit walking before?"

That was getting right to the heart of the matter. Aranloth and Kareste had both talked over the theory with her and Faran, but they had not exactly taught it. It was a thing that Ferla had not done, even once. Yet she did know the theory and she had thought she picked up a feel for it just watching Savanest.

"No. I've never done it. But I'm going to try to. What's the worst that can happen?"

They did not like it, especially Kubodin who seemed to have some knowledge of the art. But in the end, they agreed to it and let her be.

She moved away a little bit and sat down cross-legged. The others remained quiet, and gave her the peace she needed.

Slowly she breathed, focusing on the har-harat point beneath her navel. It was the center of meditation, and she felt the world slip away from her. There was just her, her slow and deep breaths and the har-harat point where the energy of her body and the magic she commanded swirled together.

After some time, she shifted the focus of her meditation. Now, she raised it to the olek-nas point between her eyebrows, what Aranloth had called the third eye.

Nothing disturbed her now, and her mind was clear as a mountain lake. No ripples moved across it. Nothing perturbed it. There was neither fear nor desire, but merely an acceptance that the world was the way it was.

Slowly, she drew her perception upward, above her body. There was a resistance, like trying to lift an object that was too heavy, but suddenly her spirit shrugged off the chains of the flesh and was weightless.

She hovered above herself, invisible and free. She had done it, and for a moment she studied her two companions. They looked not at her but at her body beneath.

It all felt strange, and doubt nagged at her. She did not really know what she was doing, but she calmed herself and set about her task.

She knew, more or less, where Savanest was, and she willed herself there. The world went dark, and there was a sensation of movement. It was disturbing, but when she stilled she could see again, despite it being night. She could see better than during the day, but all the colors seemed to be washed away from the world.

None of that mattered though. She was in Savanest's camp, and she could study it.

Nothing she saw made her feel good. Of Savanest himself, there was no sign. Why was he not here? What was he doing?

There were some fifty men. They looked hard, and there would be no mercy from them if she and her companions were caught. They seemed to her to look more like mercenaries than soldiers.

She floated above them, looking down. They were unaware of her. But there was a hound on the edge of the camp, and it growled deep in its throat and looked at her. Strange, she thought.

The beast was huge. She had never seen a dog like it before. It was thick-furred, but lean of body. Muscles rippled beneath its coat, and then there was a flash of something about its neck.

She eased closer, and the hound growled louder. The men looked at it, but said nothing. They grew uneasy though.

Surprise filled her. Around the dog's neck was a necklace. This was passingly strange, and she had never seen the like before. Tentatively, she reached out with her thought, and then instantly recoiled.

Aranloth had taught about such artifacts. A great evil he called them, and she knew now that he was right. It was a were-stone. It was a talisman of ancient magic, and it turned a man into a beast.

Swiftly she looked around, knowing what she would see. All the men wore a similar necklace. And the magic of their stones had been invoked. Already she sensed signs of the transformation that was to come, and it sickened her.

Savanest would wear a stone too. It would control the others. He was responsible for this, and that he could do such a thing was reprehensible. Few things were more evil.

She eased herself back to where the great hound stood rigidly, its legs stiff, its hackles raised and the deep growl in its throat a constant thrumming.

The truth was clear now, and with it came a sense of calm. Savanest was using the hound to track her, and that was critical to know. The beast had scented her out, and it explained why the enemy had never lost her trail despite her many tricks. She had assumed there would be a tracker, and that he must be good. But she knew better now, and that was both good and bad.

It was nearly impossible to elude a hound that tracked by scent. But at least by knowing what she was up against, she could try.

She had learned what she needed to, but she lingered, staring at the dog. Why could it sense her presence?

Strangely, the hound stepped back and whimpered. Why was it now afraid of her?

Too late she realized that it was not afraid of her at all. She made to flee back to her body, but something caught her around the legs and held her. Even as she struggled more bonds, chains of cold fire forged of sorcery, wrapped around her arms.

In a moment, unwitting and careless, she had been captured. Another chain wrapped around her neck, and then she was jerked around to look at her captor. There would be no escape now, and Savanest, a sprit figure just as herself, hovered near and smiled.

That smile was colder than the sorcery that bound her, and it sent a chill through her like ice.

"Foolish girl," Savanest said. "Did you not think I would have wards established to sense the likes of you?

Did you not think that I guessed you might try such a thing?"

16. Do You Dare?

Caludreth sat on his bed. It was clear that he had an idea how to take advantage of the mood in the city that had grown since word of his rescue had spread.

It was equally clear that Menendil would not like it. But that did not mean the idea was not good, still less that it was not necessary.

There was a knock on the door, and they both tensed instantly. The fear of discovery was on them, for they worried that at any time the king's soldiers would raid the inn having somehow learned where Caludreth was being hidden.

But there were no soldiers. It was only his old friend, Norgril, one of the very few who knew who it was hiding in the inn, and one of the very few Menendil would dare trust with that information.

Norgril caught the tension in the air. "Sorry. Only me," he said. "All is quiet downstairs."

"Pull up a chair and join us, master Norgril," Caludreth said.

The white-haired man did so, turning it around to sit in the soldier's way. His friend was no youngster anymore, but Menendil was suddenly taken back to their youth. How many times had they sat and talked exactly like this through the years? And the memory flashed to him of the semi-dark barracks where they had met the very first time one night before a mission. They had both sat just the same way then, and somehow they were still both alive, and still friends, all these years later.

Menendil saw that Caludreth was looking at him, and there was the faintest question in his eyes. He wanted to know if Norgril was trusted enough to hear the rest of the conversation he had interrupted.

With the slightest inclination of his head, Menendil signaled that he was trusted and that Caludreth should continue. At this point, it was too late to doubt that trust. Norgril already knew enough to have everyone in the inn killed and the building burned to the ground, should he speak his knowledge. But that, he would never do.

"We were just discussing," Caludreth said, "how to take advantage of the present situation. It seems my rescue has raised the spirits of the people."

"Too right it has," Norgril answered. "The city is afire with the story, and the king is in a mad rage. I've never seen Faladir in this mood before. It's ripe for trouble or rebellion. Or both."

"Then I have just the thing," Caludreth said.

Menendil wanted to hear this very much. He had tried to come up with something, but had failed. But Caludreth had once been a Kingshield Knight. What training had he had, and what tuition under a lòhren? Surely, he would suggest something good, if dangerous.

"This is what I propose," Caludreth told them. "We need to take the mood of the people, and strengthen it. To do that, we need to prove to them that there is a resistance, and that it's strong. We need to prove to them that my rescue was no accident, but the fruition of good planning." He glanced at Menendil. "Which it was, indeed."

He leaned forward in his chair. "We need to send a signal to the people that the seventh knight is coming, and that what they have seen so far is just the beginning."

Caludreth paused and looked from one to the other, and then went on.

"There's a bronze statue of the king in the city square, near the palace. You know the one I mean?"

Norgril said he knew, and Menendil nodded. He dared not speak just now.

"In that same square, there are markets every day. Thousands of people go there each morning. Few, if any places, in the city holds as many people in such a short time."

Caludreth's voice grew quiet as he spoke, and it was now barely above a whisper.

"That statue is the place to leave a message, and a message that will be seen by many. Those who see it will spread it around everywhere, and within hours no one in the city will have failed to hear it."

"What will the message be?" Norgril asked.

"First," Caludreth answered. "We will pull down the statue. That is symbolic, and the people will grasp its meaning swiftly. We need no horses for that. Ten strong men and some ropes will do the job."

Menendil immediately grasped the implications of that. It was really a direct threat to the king himself. It was a statement that not only was he defied, but that he was going to be overthrown himself. The people would see that just as quickly as he had, and the audacity of the whole thing would give it tremendous momentum. But what made it so useful also made it dangerous. Toppling the king's statue so close to the palace itself was unthinkable.

Caludreth was not done though. "When the statue is toppled, what will be left is the stone plinth. Here we can chisel some words. *The seventh knight comes*, is a phrase that might do nicely."

Silence fell, and Menendil studied the once-knight almost reverently. Here was a man who knew how to get under the skin of the enemy and rouse the people to open rebellion. But at what risk?

Caludreth looked at them both in turn. "Well, what do you think? Would you dare to attempt such a thing?"

Norgril nodded slowly, and Menendil found his voice at last.

"Do we dare not to, if we wish to see freedom in Faladir again?"

"That is exactly so," Caludreth replied, "and I'll come with you. I have a very personal grudge against the king, and this strikes to the heart of that at the same time as hitting a blow for the people."

17. A Night of Chaos

It was past the middle of the night, and the city square was devoid of people. Except for ten of the Hundred, Menendil, Caludreth and Norgril.

No one ventured abroad at night, and that was to the small party's advantage. It made it easier to move unseen, and they had passed through the dark streets without suspicion or chance of being questioned as to what they were about or why they carried ropes.

But there were disadvantages too. The reason the streets were abandoned at night was because they belonged to creatures of evil. It was not just the waylayers and murderers, though they remained. Perhaps they were driven by poverty and hunger, but Menendil did not think so. Something dark in their nature drove them, and even fear for their own lives could not subdue it.

Besides the dark element of human society, there were also the soldiers. They marched the roads, both day and night, patrolling. Or so they called it. They were dangerous during the day if someone looked at them the wrong way or made a comment they did not like. At night, they were killers. And they were not suffering hunger or poverty. The king paid them well. No, they killed for the king to instill fear in the citizens. Perhaps they killed because they liked it too. Menendil had certainly met soldiers like that back in his day, but they were the extreme exception.

But the real danger at night were the creatures of the Shadow that came out after the sun set. There were rumors of those that killed and feasted on human blood. Others bit with venom, and their victims died in agony screaming in some alley, but no one went out to help them. There were the Night Fliers too. These were the most dangerous, and Menendil had seen them himself. He preferred the name out of legend for them. Elù-draks. The names in the old stories were better, although Night Fliers was an apt description.

He had seen elù-draks on the way to the square, and he had been prepared for it. Some of the men had not seen them before though. These had nearly run, foolish as that would be. But he and Caludreth had held those firmly, and pressed them back against the side of the building they had huddled against.

There, in the shadows, they had escaped detection. But it had happened several times, and now, out in the open, their cover was gone.

But the men who had nearly panicked the first time, to Menendil's surprise, went on. He had thought they would turn back and try to go home by themselves, but they had stuck it out and their fear, while certainly not leaving them, had reduced. The subsequent time a warning had been whispered and they had pressed against the wall to hide themselves, those same men merely closed their eyes and gritted their teeth.

Menendil cast his gaze skyward as they walked across the square. The stars were dim tonight, and there was no moon to be seen. The palace hulked ahead though, on the far side of the plaza, and to the left, on the dim horizon, rose the Tower of the Stone.

The tower was several streets away. No light shone from the top, as it often did. But that did not make Menendil feel better. The heart of the evil was there, and those who had woken it might or might not be abroad. Just because there was no light did not mean the tower was empty, nor that the knights walked the streets. For that too had been rumored lately. The knights, once beacons of nobility, were said to haunt the city with the wicked things that the king had summoned to Faladir, and to join their grisly feasts. There was no proof of that, and he was inclined to disbelieve it. But who knew the truth?

They came to the statue. A grand thing it was, showing a youthful king in glory. There were other statues in the square, but this had been given pride of place at the center. It was decades old, and it was a sign of a prideful king, for he had never achieved anything special. Other kings, queens and heroes lined the sides of the square, and most of those were more loved. This was a sign that even in his youth, the king had a bad streak running through him.

They looked around. There was no sign of anyone. But even as they prepared the ropes, there was noise from the side of the square they had come from themselves. It was the sound of booted feet marching.

"Quickly!" Menendil hissed. "To the side of the square."

He raced to the side, and the men followed him. They ran, but they were careful to try to do so silently. It only took them some moments, yet it seemed an eternity. But soon they were within the deeper shadows, and huddled behind a statue of some king on a rearing horse. Menendil was not sure which one it was, for there were several such statues on this side of the square and he was disorientated in the dark, but he blessed their nameless presence and the deeper shadows they provided.

The soldiers were already in the square and they marched loudly and purposefully. It seemed though, that Menendil and his men had escaped detection. There was no sign of alarm, and the men marched directly across the square and ended up entering a street that ran into it from the other side.

The noise of the soldiers gradually receded, and soon the square was still again, as void of people as it had been when they first arrived.

"Just as well the king's men are stupid," Caludreth whispered quietly.

A few of the men sniggered, and Menendil relaxed. He knew what Caludreth had just done to relieve the tension, but in truth, stupid or otherwise, it would not take much for this mission to be revealed.

Menendil led them out again, and they acted swiftly once they reached the statue. The ropes were thrown over it, and secured in various places to offer the greatest leverage when they pulled. This was the part Menendil feared the most. When the statue was toppled, it would make a massive noise.

He glanced over at the palace. It hulked dimly in the shadows. There would be soldiers there. At least a few would be guarding the gates. Others would be sentries around the palace grounds. And inside would be hundreds. How long after the noise before they were roused?

It was reassuring to see the man chosen to carve the words nearby. He had a chisel in one hand, and a hammer in the other. He was ready to work the moment the statue came down.

Some had argued it was better to do the chiseling first. On that point, Menendil and Caludreth were of one mind. If they were interrupted and had to flee, it was better that the statue had been pulled down. That was the main message, and the words on the plinth mattered less.

Before they began to pull on the ropes though, there was movement near the palace. Three soldiers walked out, and they walked straight toward the group.

It was a tense moment. Menendil drew a knife, but hid it. Caludreth seemed relaxed. The truth was, they might have to kill these men by surprise. But that would draw more soldiers quickly. It was better to try to talk their way out of this, and just possibly that might work. The approaching soldiers clearly had no idea of what was intended, otherwise they would have alerted their comrades.

The soldiers drew near, and Menendil stepped forward, smiling. Out of the corner of his eye, he noticed Caludreth had pulled up his hood to avoid recognition. If that happened, all was lost. Yet the man was still close, and he seemed ready to spring into action. That was reassuring.

"What's going on here?" one of the soldiers demanded.

"Just what it seems," Menendil said in his friendly tone, the one he used on patrons of the inn who might cause trouble. It was easy and pleasant, but also suggested that he was in charge and knew what he was doing.

"This here statue is coming down. It's getting the chop, and a new one, twice the size, is on the way in."

The man looked at him coldly. "I've heard nothing about it."

Menendil shrugged, and left it at that. But his posture said that maybe the soldier was not as well informed as he thought he was.

The man did not like it. But he was half convinced, for who else would stand there with such confidence but someone who was doing what he was supposed to be.

"Why on earth do it at night?" one of the other soldiers asked.

It was the very question that Menendil knew would be hardest to answer, and the most dangerous if he answered wrongly.

"The way I hear it, the king thought it would be a bad look to have his statue pulled down in broad daylight. No, not a good look at all. So it was decided to do it at night, and have the new one up before the markets opened in the morning."

Menendil glanced eastward. "That won't be too far off, lads. But if you want to hold things up while you wake His Majesty … I'm happy to wait. As long as you take responsibility for the populace seeing his statue toppled, that is."

The first soldier glared at him. "Where's this new statue, then?"

"It's coming. Won't be long now," Menendil said with an easy confidence that he did not feel.

The three soldiers shuffled about uneasily. It was clear they were not sure what was happening, and that was a tremendous advantage to Menendil. Uncertainty stifled action, and so it was that the three men ended up turning and walking back toward the palace without saying another word.

"Quickly," Menendil urged his men, "let's do this now. They'll be back shortly with a senior officer and a lot more soldiers, unless I'm mistaken."

He did not think he was, nor did those around him. It had been a close call, and had they been forced to kill the soldiers an alarm would have been raised swiftly. They may not have had the time they needed to do what they intended.

The ropes pulled taught, and the men strained. Nothing happened for a moment, and then there was a groan as the bronze statue shifted on the stone plinth.

It happened slowly, but as they pulled the statue leaned precariously, and then it rapidly toppled and fell. The men drew back out of harm's way, and the thing smashed onto the cobbles of the square with a massive tumult that shattered the silence of the night.

"Pull it away!" Menendil shouted. There was no point in whispering now.

The men did so, creating quite a gap between the fallen statue and the plinth. But the man with the chisel had already leapt to work.

This would be no work of art. Nor was that needed. All that was required was that the words were legible. Swiftly the man worked, and it was hard to see in the dark. But there was light enough from the sparse starlight.

Several moments passed. There was noise from the palace, and the gate opened. Soldiers rushed through. Menendil was not sure how many, for they still seemed to be coming, but there was a dozen at least. He was about to give the order to flee, no matter that the words had not yet been fully carved, when a terrible cry tore the air. It came from above.

Menendil had only begun to look up when he heard the warnings of Night Flier and elù-drak shouted by some of the men.

He crouched down to one knee, but shifted his gaze from the sky to the palace gate instead of continuing to look up. What was happening there was what mattered most, at least for a few moments.

The soldiers, alarmed by the cry, had also crouched low in an attempt to avoid any danger. Others had retreated to the gate. None, as of yet, crossed the square.

"Keep going!" Menendil hissed at the man with the chisel. After a brief hesitation, he went back to work, and the sound of his hammer and the flying of stone chips scattering across the cobbles as they landed was loud.

There were more shouts, and Menendil, drawing his sword, looked up. Out of the dim sky a strange figure dived at them. He had never seen an elù-drak this closely before, and he wished he had not.

Like a bat it was, at least the wings. But its body was that of a naked woman's, and it screamed as it plummeted toward them.

"Do not look into its eyes!" Caludreth warned. "She can bewitch you!"

The elù-drak dived toward them, but a streak of fire leaped up to meet it. Caludreth had unleashed the magic of the knights, and the creature of the dark had not expected it. The defense was needed, but it also signaled to the soldiers near the palace that the escaped prisoner they had been seeking was here.

The Night Flier tumbled in the air, the side of her body red and blistered. But she landed on her feet, and even as she did so one hand struck out and clawed at a man's throat. A moment he stood, and then reeled away. She had crushed his windpipe, and the sound of his rasping breath and the blood that bubbled from his ruined neck showed that she had killed him, even if he was not dead quite yet.

Menendil charged at her with his sword. But Caludreth was quicker. He thrust the tip of the blade in her belly, and Menendil hacked at her head but struck her shoulder instead.

The creature of the dark screamed, but it would take more than this to kill her. She reeled back, blood running from her gut wound, but she did not retreat.

Even as she stepped back, she moved to the side and with a beat of her wings launched herself full at Caludreth from a different angle.

Some of the other men had joined the fray now, and swords struck and stabbed at her. More blood flowed, but it was hard to strike her and not Caludreth at the same time, for she had crashed into him, her hands straining to reach his neck.

On the ground the two combatants fell, rolling and vying for life and death. Her hands reached for his throat, and he had dropped his sword, useless as it was to him in this position, and fended her deadly grip away.

By some exertion of tremendous strength, the once-knight got one leg under himself and managed to drive himself up and fling her away. She careered backward, twisted as she reeled, and tried to take flight. But the men were onto her, swords flashing and stabbing.

Blood spurted, and she screamed. It was not a scream of pain, but of shear hatred, and she launched into the men knocking several over. The ones that were still upright began to scatter, but just then Caludreth returned to the fray and fire spurted again from his fingers. Like strands of rope the flames were, and they wrapped around her legs and climbed upward engulfing her in an inferno.

She was not done though, and Menendil feared she could never be killed. She came at Caludreth, fire twining up her body and sparking in her hair. Her hands reached for him, but one of the men struck her from behind and she stumbled.

Caludreth had used up all his strength in magic, or else he trusted more to steel and skill at arms. His sword flashed through the air in a mighty blow and hewed her head off her neck.

Still the body came tumbling at him, and he kicked it away. The head rolled over the cobbles, and Menendil thought even now he saw her eyes fixed on the once-knight in hatred as her hair fully caught alight.

A terrible stench filled the air, and Menendil fought off the urge to vomit. He glanced over at the palace gate and saw that the soldiers were gathering there, and there were more of them. With the creature dead, it would not be long before they raced out.

His glance also took in the work the man with the chisel had done. *The seventh knight comes* was carved there in large letters. It was easily visible by the light of the burning corpse, and very soon daylight would reveal it to the world.

Their work was done, and all that remained now was to flee.

"Get home, boys!" he cried, and at his word they turned and ran.

One they left behind, and he was dead. But the others scattered to all corners of the square, for there were alleys and streets that ran onto it from many places.

Menendil raced over the cobbles. He was not a fast runner, and the others that had gone this way were ahead of him. Behind him he heard a clamor of shouting and knew the soldiers had hastened into action and were in pursuit.

It was not that though that sent a shiver of fear stabbing through him. From above, came that terrible but now familiar cry. Another elù-drak.

Menendil looked upward, and the thing hurtled from the sky at him. He dived and rolled. At least he tried to, but he was not as young as he was. Somehow he cracked his head against the cobbles.

His fall might have saved him, for he remained low to the ground. The creature passed over, but even as he tried to stagger to his feet a wave of dizziness washed over him.

Desperate, sword in hand, he ran for the street that he had been hoping to escape down, but blood dripped in his eyes from a gash he had not realized he had, and somehow he came to the wall of a building. He turned to his right, wiping the blood away, but even as the street opening beckoned he saw this new elù-drak land in front of him, blocking off his route.

She advanced, naked and terrible, her wings outstretched like shadows behind her, her chest heaving for breath and death in her wicked eyes.

Almost, Menendil hoped the soldiers would arrive to capture and save him, but from the corner of his eye he saw that they had halted again. They dared not approach.

He was going to die here, alone and unaided, for all his men had scattered and were gone. Not that he blamed them, and two deaths for what they had achieved this night was a small price to pay.

18. You are Mine

Ferla cursed her stupidity. She had allowed herself to be taken, and she had never felt such fear in her life.

The bonds of magic burned into her spirit form like lashes from a whip. They were like fire, if fire could burn as ice.

Worse though was her humiliation. Bound, taunted and unable to fight back. She was at Savanest's mercy, and she knew he had none.

His spirit form reached out and traced a cold hand down her cheek.

"You're pretty, for a knight. But a knight doesn't need good looks."

She was not sure if that were a threat, but it could not really be taken any other way. For the first time, she wondered if injuries received during spirit walking could appear on her real body. How little she knew of the magic she had invoked, and how foolish she had been to invoke it without proper knowledge.

Savanest looked deep into her eyes. "I see your fear, girl. You cannot hide it. You can hide nothing from me, for I own you now. You are mine, now and forever. I will treat you as I will, and you will learn to beg for a good word from me."

He paused and considered her. "Would you like to learn that now? Will you beg for my favor now, or must I break you first?"

His eyes gazed deep into hers. "It may be that I will enjoy breaking you."

Ferla's fear redoubled. His words were bad enough, but in defiance she did not look away from his terrible glance. And she saw something in it that forced panic to rise up inside her.

Savanest's pupils were large and dark, but it seemed to her that she saw something more. She saw, in each eye, the black Morleth Stone. She felt the power of it, and the unnamed sorceries that churned within.

And she felt the will of the artifact. It was alive, and it thought, and considered and plotted. She felt it stir, and it began to reach out to her.

All her fears from before had been as nothing. Now, she understood what it intended. It would bend her to its will. It would make her a Morleth Knight, and she would betray her friends, and Faran, and all Alithoras. She would be turned to evil, and she would know but be unable to halt her actions.

Savanest laughed softly, and she felt his spirit-breath upon her face.

"Welcome to your future, sister knight. The glory of serving the Morleth Stone, of serving Osahka, will be yours. And with it, the torment. It will never cease. Each day it will grow stronger. You will yearn for death, but you will taste of life everlasting, and despair."

Ferla already felt despair. It bound her more strongly that Savanest's sorcery. Her future was not her own. Her life was a plaything for the evil in the world. Desperately, she sought a means of escape. She wondered what Aranloth would do, for certainly he would never have been caught by his own stupidity in such a trap.

She remembered their many lessons, and their times together in the pursuit of knowledge and mastery. She remembered, and even as her mind reached out toward those memories, it seemed to her that she sensed his mind somewhere far away.

It was both dark and light where he was. There was magic, and the touch of the void that once she had walked. It was hardly less fearful than what she experienced here, and yet over the vast gulf between them his words brushed against her mind.

Flee! he commanded. *All is illusion. Flee!*

Her mind lurched back to where she was. Aranloth's voice was urgent, if it were his voice at all and not some delirium caused by fear, but it was also reassuring.

Yet how was it possible to flee when she was bound?

Frustration welled up within her, but she beat it down even as she beat down the fear. She must think.

And then she had it. In one swift thought she realized all. This was the spirit world, and all was illusion. Just as when she had walked the void once before when she had been poisoned and near to death, and learned that thought was action. Thought was reality. Thought ruled perception. By accepting that the bonds placed on her by Savanest were real, she had made them so.

With a primal shout that was not of words but relief and triumph and hope all at once, she shrugged off the fetters of fire as though they were but strings.

Savanest recoiled, and a look of incredulity was on his face. Fast as an arrow sped from a bow she flew toward where her body rested far away. Yet the voice of the Morleth Knight shadowed after her.

As it was in the world of spirit, so too will it be in the world of flesh. You are mine, and you will know it when next we meet.

She heard those words, and they filled her with dread. Yet she was free now, and with a rush she filled her body. Shuddering, she came awake and leaped up, drawing her sword.

Asana and Kubodin were startled. They had been nearby, watching her. She knew they saw the naked fear on her face, and that embarrassed her.

"I should not have gone," she whispered, sheathing her sword. Then she looked at her arms. They were unblemished, yet still she felt the memory of pain.

19. A Worthy Foe

Druilgar stood atop the Tower of the Stone, and he surveyed his realm.

The night was old, and from his vantage he saw the slow graying of the eastern sky. Dawn was not far off. Yet still the night was dark. He had communed earlier with the Morleth Stone, and he knew that another kind of dawn was not far away. This one would herald an epoch of reason. The new age was coming, and the world would be reordered. Justice would prevail. The laws of all lands would be right and proper. The past would be erased, so that it would not blight the glorious future.

He would be the sun of that new world, and he felt the burden of it. His would be the responsibility to ensure it came to pass, and it was humbling.

Never had he been humbler in his life. He served a greater purpose now, and if it bestowed everlasting glory upon him, and raised him above humanity, then so be it. What he would do, and what he would achieve, was all to serve the Great Purpose, and not himself.

Lights glimmered all over Faladir. There were lamps in streets, and within windows. But better was the dark expanse of the shadowed areas of the city, enveloped in murk and the beauty of mystery. Dark were the alleys, and even whole suburbs where the poorer citizens dwelt were draped by unrelieved night. There, his servants found nourishment. They did not like the light. Not yet. But their day was coming, too. For they served the Great Purpose, as did he. They would be raised even as he would.

The time of reckoning was coming, and the world would be washed clean.

At last, he saw what he had been waiting for. An elùdrak sped through the night. It was a thing of perfect beauty. Its thin body glistened palely against the dark beat of its graceful wings. It glided toward the tower, dropping height and alighting with confidence upon a merlon of the parapet.

She stood there, and she fixed him with her eyes. He smiled at that. The creatures possessed a natural magic. With their eyes they could seduce and make a man kill himself. She was testing him now.

He understood the lure, too. She was a thing of beauty unsurpassed, and her eyes gazed into his and he felt the fire of her magic. Those were eyes to gaze into, too. They promised so much, and yet held mystery.

But he was immune to that magic. Osahka had granted him power over them rather than them power over him. He was in command, and they obeyed. Or they were punished.

"Speak," Druilgar commanded.

"I have flown widely," she answered, "and hunted far."

Her voice was soft and alluring also. Many had thought the creatures could not speak, but he had known better. They spoke to those who controlled them, but seldom to their victims.

"From the west I have come, and Knight Sofanil I have conversed with."

"What did he say?"

"He had no message. None other than what you already know. He continues to search."

"And what of Savanest?"

"He, I have not spoken to. But Sofanil says his brother has found a treasure of old. A hoard of were-stones, and with them he better controls his men. Sofanil believes he does not quite understand the magic and underestimates the influence of the stones."

That was news, and Druilgar considered it. Were-stones were not the first of the ancient talismans to be found. Likely they would not be the last. The Morleth Stone was at work there, and he sensed it trying to rebuild the old world as it had been. It was like a man trying to rebuild a house that had blown down in a storm. All the pieces were there. They just needed gathering and bringing back together again.

He studied the creature before him. She was something of the kind, too. The Morleth Stone drew creatures from hiding and from sleep that had not walked, or flown, the world for millennia. Where they had hidden, he did not know. But the world was full of them, and he was pleased.

"Go find nourishment," Druilgar told her. "Report again tomorrow night, and I will have new orders for you."

She grinned at him, and gazed deep into his eyes. It mattered not to her where that nourishment came from.

"Be off," he commanded. Her magic had no power over him, but they all tested that.

"It will be as you wish, master."

Despite her words, he still sensed her hunger for him. He could never trust these creatures, but they had their uses.

After a moment, she turned her sleek body and dived off the parapet, winging away into the dark.

It would not be long before the next appeared. They did not like to see each other, at least up close, and always reported separately.

Druilgar waited and mused. The knights were his to command, and his was the greater power by far. Yet still he must watch them. He trusted them no more than an elù-drak, and any one of them would supplant him if they could.

He did not like them gaining in power. Especially, he did not like it when that power did not come from him. But the world moved on, and the more power they had the more they sought. Yet he alone could hold the Morleth Stone. Osahka promised him preeminence, and in that promise he trusted. The stone was all that he believed in now, and he was right to bind himself to it. It was the future.

A dark figure swept through the air near the tower, and there was a rush of wings. It was gone into the night again, and then it banked back, swept lower and alighted with grace on the parapet near him.

This elù-drak was younger. She had not the confidence of the previous one, but still those eyes locked onto his and he took a step forward before he controlled himself.

"Speak!" he ordered.

The creature gave what might have been a bow. "The lands of the north and west I have flown," she replied. "My belly is full, and my eyes have seen much. My ears also have heard the tidings of the land."

Druilgar knew what that meant. She had taken a man captive and made him into her thrall. Off him, she had gathered news. And then she had killed him. The magic did not last long.

"What tidings have you heard?"

She told him many things then, some of which he knew already and others that were new. For the most part, it was good news.

He questioned her most about the city of Cardoroth, then he bid her go. She did not need to eat, but like a cat hunting a mouse for the play of it, she would find amusement in the streets below.

Cardoroth interested him, and greatly. He had heard much before, but he knew more now.

It was a weak city, at the moment. The old king was gone, and a new king was in his place. War had ravished the realm. It was ripe for the plucking, and more and more Druilgar considered that it would be his first target. It was not that far away, and he could establish good supply routes for an army. His army was both fresh and growing. There would be little battle. Like fire engulfing a forest, his new order would overrun the target. Then, he would sit on two thrones, and he could contemplate the next move.

It was rumored though that the new king in Cardoroth was a lòhren-king. He was aided by lòhrens, and he was one himself. That was a factor to consider. So too that he had so far overcome all obstacles in his path.

But in the end, all men encountered forces they could not beat. This new king would find it so, for lòhren or not, he had no aid from a Morleth Stone. He would be a worthy foe, and then he would fall before bright steel or dark sorcery. It mattered not which.

Druilgar had not long to wait before a third elù-drak reported. This one was older, yet she approached with sublime grace. She banked at an angle, and then glided to land before him.

Like all the others, she held him with her gaze, testing him. But in her wisdom she knew in but a moment that he would not succumb.

"From the south I have come," she said, and her voice was deeper and richer than the previous ones. "It is home to my kind, and all is well there."

"You saw nothing of interest?"

"Nothing did I see save that the land stirs and allies of old wake. More of my kind will come, and others also that serve the Shadow. You have friends, great one, and they come to support you. Of enemies, I saw none."

He sent her away then. Her news was good, and expected. The elù-draks had been the first to serve, for they had the power of flight and could cover great distances. Yet he longed for the day that other soldiers would swell his army, and it mattered little if they were not human. All could serve equally, and all be equally honored.

Dawn was close at hand now. He should return to the palace and sleep a little, though he had less need for it now. The Morleth Stone seemed to sustain him more and more. Yet he reveled in the night, and enjoyed the blanket of darkness. Below him, that dark was lit by lights just as the sky was lit by stars, but here, in Faladir, he was in control. Sometimes, he felt the stars mocked him.

He was nearly ready to descend the tower, but something stayed him. He gazed around, for the vantage of the pinnacle of the tower offered him a view of the entire city.

Something was wrong, and he waited.

But not for long. There was a mighty crash that came from nearby, somewhere in the People's Square. There was a commotion there, and he knew by instinct, or magic, that it was the work of rebels.

With his mind he summoned the elù-draks that he had so recently spoken to. Two of them came and alighted before him, ignoring each other. The third was some distance away, but he sensed her speeding toward him.

He pointed to the square. "There is trouble there," he said. "Kill our enemies! And when you are done, spread terror through the city. Let the people, let all who dwell here, know fear!"

The creatures dove from the top of the tower and sped into the dark. They would see his will done, and he would watch and listen.

Yet still it disturbed him. How could there be rebels? And greatest of them Caludreth who had escaped. He was a threat, if ever there was one.

Anger burned through him. Fury even. He had thought himself above emotions, but perhaps this night would subdue the city once and for all.

20. Like His Own Shadow

The middle reaches of the night had passed, and Savanest sat alone in thought.

He had much to think about, for much had happened.

His mind turned to the girl. He was fascinated by her. How had she learned the magic she had in such a short time? It was clear that she had talent, but that was not enough. Nor did she have the Morleth Stone to nurture her, as did he.

It was a problem that he could not solve. Far better to just accept, however it was done, that she had learned swiftly what it had taken him a lifetime to discover. What had taken him decades had taken her just the passing of a few seasons.

So it was also with her skill at fighting. That, he had not seen himself yet. But he had seen Lindercroft's grave. That was proof enough.

But her skills, however acquired, were not really an issue. Still less a problem. Her, and her ragtag group of followers were not a match for his force. If it had been necessary, he would have summoned more aid before he moved on her. But it was not necessary, and doing so would have carried risks.

He did not know exactly where Sofanil was. But he would not share credit for the girl's capture with him. It was possible other knights had been sent also. He could not be sure, but he did not think so.

No. The girl would be his, and he would take her in fetters before the king. He would be rewarded for that, though certainly it would be reward enough to see her taken to the holy presence of the Morleth Stone, and look into her eyes as she was transformed against her will. The moment of her breaking would be exquisite.

He could barely wait for that moment, and that it was some while away only enhanced his expectations. But her capture was not that far off. It would be soon, and he had already placed his mark upon her. Fear gripped her, and like a leash he would pull that and control her. When the time came she would be powerless against him.

His was the greater power, and she knew that now. She had seen, perhaps, the Morleth Stone. It was always on his mind, and even as he had gazed into her eyes he had felt the stone stir and reach toward her. She knew what was coming, and against that she could not prevail.

Or maybe it was just his fancy that she had seen the stone through his gaze. He himself saw it all the time now, so it was only natural that he would assume she saw it too. But he had not imagined its stirring.

For a moment, he felt uneasy. Why should he see the stone at all times? He was a knight, after all, and he was in charge of his own destiny. He did not need the stone.

Even as he thought that, the image of the stone rose unbidden in his mind. Black it was, mysterious as the midnight sky. What forces did it contain, hidden? What powers that could change the world?

It was a thing of beauty, too. Black, polished to a smoothness like glass, yet harder than diamond. He laughed then, remembering how they had beat at him with hammers, cast him from the heights onto the stones below, buried him in the depths of furnaces and smote him with magic. Yet he still lived, as he always would. Life eternal was his.

Savanest swayed and felt a roar in his ears. No, that was not him. That was the Morleth Stone. That was what they had done to it in ages past to destroy it. And they had failed.

The wave of dizziness faded. He was himself again, but the stone remained on his mind. It was with him always, like his own heartbeat, breath or shadow.

He bestirred himself. Too long he had thought. It was time for action, and he knew what needed doing. Dawn was creeping over the land, and his men would be awake. For them, it would be a day like no other.

The camp was astir when he walked into it. The men had eaten, or were just finishing their meal. There were campfires, and these were being put out. They were not great soldiers, but they were organized. He could say that much for them, but they needed to be more, and they would be.

He waited until they were done, and the captain approached him.

"What orders, my lord."

"We will continue the hunt. While you slept, I have communed with our quarry."

"You found her camp?" the captain asked.

"She found ours," Savanest replied, and he knew all the men had gathered close and were listening intently.

"She was here, while we slept?"

"In a manner of speaking. But do not fear, she could do you no harm. I was here to protect you."

"And you spoke with her?"

"Indeed I did, and it was a pleasant conversation. At least for me. She, on the other hand, would not be so pleased. I put fear upon her such as she has never felt before."

The captain shaded his eyes from the rising sun. "Will she not try all the harder to flee from us, then?"

Savanest grinned. "But of course, yet what does that matter?" He pointed to the were-hound that sat on its haunches near the men, its head tilted and its ears pricked, listening.

"We have the means to find her anywhere, now. But we still must be quick."

Gently, Savanest touched the were-stone about his neck and pulsed magic into it. He felt a moment of uncertainty about what he was doing, but then he pushed it aside. Necessity demanded the action he would take.

"Men," he said. "You have served me well. And I know you have more yet to give. Are you ready to serve your king and realm?"

The captain saluted. "I'm ready, my lord!"

There were shouts from the soldiers as well, but not all of them.

Savanest infused more magic into the stone, and he sent it out like ripples in a pond to all the other stones.

"Are you ready, men?" he asked again.

This time there was a roar of approval. But the hound that had once been a man began to growl. No one paid it any heed.

Again, Savanest sent a pulse of magic through the stone. Rarely had he ever held such power. His strength was growing day by day. Whether it was enhanced by the Morleth Stone or the controlling were-stone that he wore about his own neck, he did not know. But he liked it.

"Let the world tremble!" he cried out. "For we are coming!"

"We are coming!" the men shouted back. They stamped their boots and clapped their hands. Some lifted high their heads and unleashed a primal sound that contained no words but spoke of their eagerness.

Savanest surveyed them. They were almost a pack of wolves preparing to set out on a hunt, and he laughed. But he concentrated once more.

One last pulse of magic he sent through the stone about his neck and into the others. One last invocation of power, and the change would begin and nothing could stop it.

The captain screamed first. He drew his sword, but only looked at it in bewilderment. Then he screamed again and cast the blade aside. He had no use for it anymore.

Or perhaps it was because his fingers grew together, and fur sprouted down his arms. He screamed again, though maybe it was a howl.

Rolling to the ground, the captain moaned and frothed at the mouth. But his mouth disappeared as a snout grew. Wicked teeth gleamed as the lips were pulled back, and the eyes darkened to deep pits of animalistic hatred.

He knew what had been done to him, at least that part of him that retained human thought and emotion, but that did not matter. He must obey the stone he wore.

But still he thrashed on the ground. Fur sprouted everywhere over his skin, and his body changed, stretching and altering shape. The clothes he wore split, and he bit and chewed at the leather belt that his sword sheath hung from. With a snarl, he bit through it, and then snapped at the boots that hung in tatters around his lengthened paws.

The captain was soon gone, and a were-hound rose to all fours in his place.

Savanest looked around. Of the soldiers that had faced him before, he now saw his new servants. Or at least the beginnings of what they would be. Many had stayed mostly human, but all showed some sign of the change. They waked on two legs, yet snouts had grown on some. On others, tufted ears stood out. Some had the round shoulders of bears, while the bristled skin and tusks of boars stood out on others.

With the last of his magic, Savanest infused the stones they wore with a final surge of power. This would give them endurance and speed to run. Then he drew on the magic to sustain himself so that he could keep up with them.

He looked at the tracker hound that had watched all this and whimpered. Was he glad now to have companions?

With a surge of thought through the stone, he told the hound what he wanted, and it leaped to the chase. The hunt was on now in earnest, and Ferla would learn even greater fear.

21. A Debt Repaid

The elù-drak approached, and Menendil held his sword in a trembling grip. He had heard the legends, and just before he had heard Caludreth's warning. *Do not look into her eyes.*

But he could not help himself. Like water that must run downhill, his gaze met her own against his will.

And she smiled at him. She was beautiful. She was everything he had ever desired. In her arms…

He looked away, and there was a hiss from the creature. She was not as beautiful now, and the lips that once held promises were pulled back to reveal gleaming teeth, but it was no smile.

"Back!" he cried, and he waved his sword threateningly. All his wits and skill with a blade seemed to have deserted him, but at least he was avoiding that deadly gaze.

"Come to me," she whispered, and stepped closer.

He would rather have fled, but he knew that if he did so she would be on his back quicker than thought, teeth biting and hands ripping.

"Come to me," she implored again, and there was a note of disappointment in her voice. Perhaps she sensed that having nearly succumbed to her once, but resisting, he would not easily fall victim to her lure a second time.

Nor would he. He strengthened his will. If he were to die here, at least it would be fighting and not as a slave to her.

The fighting would come soon, for she spoke no more and stalked toward him. Her every move was grace, and the wings behind her flared a little at each step. She almost floated toward him, part walking and part flying.

He saw the wicked spurs at the elbow joints of her wings, and he concentrated on these, shifting his gaze from one to the other so as not to look into her eyes.

It was the spurs that were his greatest danger. Almost, he fancied, he could see the deadly poison they contained glisten on their surface. One scratch from those and he would be finished.

She came at him in a rush. With a snarl and flaring wings she attacked, but he was ready for it. He drove his sword forward in a lunge.

The elù-drak was swift though. She dodged to the side, avoiding the tip of his sword, and came at him from an angle. He retreated, nearly tripping in his haste. But somehow he got his blade between the two of them, and she paused.

He was no match for her. She was too fast, and would have probably been so in his youth. He had practiced little with the blade these last few years, and his skill had fallen away from him like leaves off an autumnal tree in the first gale of winter.

What could he do? Nothing. He would die here, but he would do so with dignity. He would be no thrall to her magic, and if he could, he would take her with him.

He drew his dagger, so that if she got past the sword, which she would, even as he died he would stab her. Perhaps it would be a mortal blow, and perhaps not. But he would likely only get one chance.

Yet the dagger was long, and he saw her wicked gaze fall to it. She had read his mind, and her eagerness had lessened. But in the end, it would not stop her. It would only make her more careful.

Menendil decided on something. While she hesitated, it was time for him to act. It was an old lesson from his army days. Do what the enemy expects least, especially when you are outmatched.

He lunged toward her, this time not stabbing but slashing in a narrow range of movement, always keeping the sword between them and never overextending.

She seemed surprised, and she rose up slightly in the air as her wings beat rapidly, but she avoided him with ease and landed some distance away.

Menendil slowed, now stepping forward with careful steps, stalking her as she had stalked him only moments before.

She tilted her head and gazed at him, her tongue sliding across her lips.

"Come to me, little man," she said. "You are a worthy opponent. I will reward you. Kneel before me. Worship me, and you will live. I promise it."

Menendil felt his legs go weak. He knew it was her magic at work, and he knew she would kill him despite her words, but the force of her will was overpowering.

He was not sure what he would have done. The strength of her will was like a wave washing over him, but the burning desire to live was just as strong. He stood, trembling and uncertain, the sword in his hand nearly forgotten.

But suddenly the force of her will was gone, and she turned her head to the side. Even as she did so, a blast of fire washed over her, and Caludreth came running, sword in hand and attacked her.

Abruptly free of indecision, Menendil also attacked. Even as the creature turned away from him to face the greater threat, he drove his sword into her.

It was not a killing blow. His thrust was not well directed, and it took her at the top of her hip and careered off the bone. Yet still she screamed, and her eyes flashed hatred at him like fiery daggers.

That was a mistake, for she took her eyes off Caludreth, and his blow was better. It was aimed at her neck, intended to sever her head from her body. But at the last moment her wings rose and the elbow joint came forward as she twisted. The blow hit her there, and then skidded to strike the top of her head.

The elù-drak swayed, made dizzy by the force of the blow. Menendil struck again, trying to do what Caludreth had attempted, and decapitate her, but she ducked and rolled, coming to her feet some distance away, and then with a beat of her wings lifted skyward.

She was safe from swords, but not from magic. A streak of fire burst forth again, and it took her in the head. Her hair caught fire, and with a scream and great beats of her wings she rose swiftly high above the square and disappeared behind some buildings.

Menendil did not look at Caludreth. His eyes flickered toward the soldiers. They remained some distance away, unsure if the creature would come back. But their leader turned to them and seemed about to give a signal to attack.

Caludreth raised both arms, the sword in one. But it was not a gesture designed for fighting. Truly, Menendil thought, the arts of the knights were wonderous.

Fog rose from the cobbles, and swirled toward the soldiers. They backed away, and even as they did so the whole square seemed to fill with mist deeper and thicker than Menendil had ever seen.

He looked at Caludreth in amazement, but he saw the knight was swaying. Swiftly he went to him and put an arm around his shoulder to steady him. Whatever marvelous skills he possessed, they did not come without cost.

Awkwardly, the once-knight sheathed his blade. "We have to hurry," he said. "The fog won't last long."

They hastened away then, each supporting the other. But Caludreth seemed to gain strength at every step, and he needed no more help by the time they passed through the street that Menendil had hoped to use earlier.

The fog disappeared quickly too. It must still fill the square, but Caludreth had not conjured it over a wide area. Here, the night was clear, and the sky was open above.

They crossed another street quickly, then headed through an alley. Back and forth they zigzagged, making sure that there was no chance they could be run down. But soon they slowed. Two factors asserted themselves.

The first was that there was no sound of pursuit. They had evaded the soldiers. That should have brought relief, but the second became more urgent. Now that they had no need to hasten so much, they had more time to think of the elù-drak.

"Do you think she'll leave us alone?" Menendil asked.

Caludreth knew exactly who he meant. "Not her. She was hurt, but not killed. Those things are very hard to kill. Very, very hard. She's out there somewhere, and the pain I inflicted would have receded. No doubt, she's already looking for us again."

It was not reassuring, but Menendil felt almost safe in the other man's presence. Between them both, and the magic the once-knight possessed, they might survive an attack.

They turned another corner, and now they were getting close to the inn and safety.

"You came back for me," Menendil said. "Thank you for that."

It seemed a poor way of saying thanks to the man who had saved his life, but it was all he could think of.

Caludreth grinned at him. His face was clear now, for the dawn was at hand. It was still dark, but only a twilight sort of darkness. Day would be swift in coming now, and they must find shelter soon. They could not risk Caludreth being recognized on the streets.

"Of course I came back for you," the once-knight answered. "You rescued me from a fate worse than any elù-drak, so I still owe you."

"That debt is repaid now," Menendil replied. "Well and truly. Faladir needs you. It doesn't need me, so the risk you took was greater than the risk I took for you."

"I do not see it so," the big man replied. "None of this would have happened without you. Your service to Faladir has been greater than my own."

Menendil did not think so, but this was no time to debate the matter. Already there were a few people in the street forced out on some urgent errand. They seemed hesitant, and well they might be. They could not have missed the terrible cries from not long ago. They would know what creatures were abroad in this part of the city. But daylight was safe, and daylight was at hand.

They kept their distance from the few people they saw, pretending to be just like them and hurrying on some pressing task that could not wait.

"How did you even know I needed help?" Menendil asked.

Caludreth glanced skyward, as they both were doing incessantly.

"I thought as we ran from the statue that you were close behind me. I was wrong though, and I was well down a street before I realized it. I turned to speak to you, and found it was another of the Hundred instead."

The once-knight paused as a man came from a building nearby. He glanced at them, then looked skyward and walked to the other side of the street to avoid them.

Caludreth continued. "I hesitated then, unsure what to do or where you were. Then I heard the cry of an elù-drak from back in the square, and I knew."

Menendil realized just how much his life had hung on a thread. Had Caludreth ignored the cry, which no one would have blamed him for, Menendil would not be alive to hear this conversation.

He sighed, and then looked up out of nervousness. Even as he did so, he saw a shadow plummet silently toward them, all pale body and dark wings. With a sudden move, he pushed Caludreth over and sprawled to the ground himself.

The shadow passed over them, and there was a rush of air that Menendil felt across his skin. It gave him the shivers.

But a moment later they were up and running. The buildings helped them here, for they prevented the creature from seeing them at times or launching an attack from most angles.

They disappeared down an alley, and it was one Menendil knew very well. They were close to The Bouncing Stone now, but no matter how close he would not enter its safety while there was a chance of being seen. He would bring no danger down on his wife or staff.

There was no rush of wings for the next attack. The creature did not fly but crawled down a wall toward them. It had done so silently and was nearly upon them when Caludreth cried out.

"Close your eyes!" he ordered. A moment Menendil hesitated, but against all instincts he did as Caludreth asked.

There was a mighty flash of light that burned like the sun even through Menendil's eyelids, then there was a scream. The creature fell from the wall.

"Run!" Caludreth commanded. And they ran. They crossed a street and went down another alley, and then suddenly they were at the back door of the inn.

"It's blinded for a few moments," Caludreth hissed. "Quickly. Let's get inside while we can."

Menendil glanced around once more, making sure they were not observed by anyone. Then he opened the door and closed it quickly behind them.

They were safe again, if safety existed any longer in Faladir.

22. We Cannot Hide

Ferla slept, but it would only be a short rest. Dawn was approaching, and then they must be on the move again.

Her sleep was disturbed. Dark dreams threaded through it, and the touch of Savanest's phantom hand always seemed to be on her skin. He had said she would be his, but she rejected that. Better to die than become what he wanted.

She woke with the morning sun on her face. Asana and Kubodin were already up, and they had prepared breakfast.

She did not much feel like eating.

"Food is medicine," Kubodin encouraged her. They did not know all that had happened last night, nor all that was said. But they were both shrewd and knew the gist of things and could piece more together.

She ate then, but having started she found that she was indeed hungry. Kubodin watched her with a knowing look, while a little way away Asana practiced a sword form, his every movement pure grace.

She finished eating, and they were ready to leave when she halted them.

"A moment," she said, and she saw concern in their eyes.

"Savanest will begin the hunt now, and nothing will stop him. We know now how he keeps finding us, and I don't see a way to prevent him."

They both looked at her earnestly, but said nothing.

She went on, steeling herself for what she must say. Wishing that it were otherwise, but knowing it was not.

"It's me he hunts. Only me. You two can get away, and you should."

They looked at her solemnly. But it was Asana who spoke.

"We thought you would suggest something like this. We discussed it last night after you slept. And we are both in agreement."

"In agreement about what?"

"We're not going anywhere, except with you," Kubodin said. "We made our decision on the mountain, and we knew this would come."

But not so soon, Ferla thought. She did not say it. Instead, she just looked at them, and felt an enormous sense of gratitude. For all the problems and the evil in the world, it was good for this. True friends who would stand with her, no matter what. Yet still, if something happened to them, she would feel guilty.

She surprised even herself then, and hugged them. She would not argue against their decision.

"Then let us be away," she said. If they must endure danger by being with her, then at least she could do whatever was possible to protect them. And the sooner they were on the move again, the safer they would be.

They headed off. As usual, she led them, and she employed all the skills she possessed to try to hide their trail. But where they were now, this was not easy, nor would it fool a hound who hunted them by scent. So, while she tried various things, she mostly spent her time finding the easiest trail ahead. That would spare their energy, and perhaps keep them ahead of the enemy.

Alithoras was alive around her as she walked. Perhaps it was the fear of impending death, or worse. Perhaps it was the joy of traveling new lands that she had never seen before. But she loved the grassy slopes and the little forests, no bigger than a farm was back in Dromdruin. She loved it all, and she breathed deep of the fresh air and luxuriated in the wilderness. There was no evidence of long-ago battles. She saw nothing that even indicated people had lived here. Ever. The land was wild and free.

They passed by herds of aurochs, grazing on the verge of woodlands. Hawks hovered in the air, gliding to unseen currents and remaining almost motionless except for their heads that swiveled from side to side searching for food. In patches of bare dirt, she saw the tracks of a badger and a fox.

All around the grass was green and lush, and even as she smelled a strong scent and recognized it, a covey of quail burst from nearly underfoot and hurled themselves with a whoosh of wings in the air. They did not fly far, but landed in cover again.

Her heart raced, and it kept racing as they walked. It was no time for surprises, but the wild was like that. Those who traveled in it got used to its ways, and accepted them. Just as they accepted the dangers. They could break a leg far from home, or twist an ankle or fall down a steep embankment. But those risks were worth it, many times over.

She thought of Faran, and wished he could see this land. He would like it. She wondered where he was. He could not be that far away yet. Perhaps where he was, it was similar to this.

At least he was not in danger though. That was a thought that gave her strength. Savanest had come after her, and whatever came of that Faran would be safe. So as much as it hurt to be away from him, it gave her joy as well.

They moved down a slope, angling their way along a gulley, and the sun warmed their backs. She had changed the direction of their normal travel.

Asana drew level with her. "What are we looking for, Ferla."

She could see in his eyes that he had guessed the answer.

"I'm hoping to find a good place to defend. We cannot hide, for the were-hound will find my scent."

Asana was not surprised. She had been right, and he knew. But he was wise enough to explore all options first before committing to that.

"What if we found water though? A creek or a stream does not seem unlikely in this land."

That was certainly true. And earlier she had wished just that herself. But then she had considered her way through it.

"In the past," she replied, "I have used water to hide our trail. But it didn't work, did it?"

Asana frowned at that. It was something he had not realized before. She could not blame him for that. She was the one with the tracking skills, and the better knowledge of the wild. She glanced at Kubodin though, and saw that he knew.

"How could the were-hound follow a scent through water?"

"It's widely believed," Ferla said, "that water can hide your trail. But it's a myth."

Asana raised an eyebrow.

"It's true," Ferla continued. "Walking through a body of water can fool a human tracker. At least sometimes. A human tracker relies on eyesight and spotting the trail. The better ones can get inside the mind of those they track as well, figuring out intuitively what choices they might make."

"But a dog?" Asana asked.

"A dog tracks by scent. Each of us leave our scent behind wherever we go, and that includes in water. If we were in steep country, and found fast running water somewhere, maybe we could use that. But we'll have no such luck here. Yet even with swift-running water, a dog would just pick our scent up on the other side."

They kept walking, and Asana thought on what she said.

"It's not really possible to evade them then?"

Ferla shook her head. "Not really. Not by hiding our trail or scent. Hounds just can't be fooled that way. There is another way, but it won't work for us."

"What other way is that?"

"We could try to outrun them, for a fit human can do so over a long distance and tire the dog out. We might just be fit enough to do that, but not in armor and carrying weapons."

"You know a lot about this," Asana said.

"Tracking and hunting is not much different from fighting. They are all skills, and if you practice and have good teachers you can learn a lot that most don't know."

They came out of the gully and walked over a flat area, although the land rose ahead of them again in another slope.

"I assume," Kubodin said, "that you've dismissed the idea of leaving our weapons behind and running?"

He looked like he hoped very much that that was the case.

"I have. All our weapons and armor mean too much to us. But more importantly, running is not certain to bring us to safety. And if not, what then? We would still end up facing the enemy, but would be defenseless against them."

They tackled the slope ahead of them, moving up swiftly with long strides. Kubodin dismounted from his mule, giving the animal a chance to climb without carrying extra weight.

"Then there's nothing for it but to do as you suggest. We have to find a place where we can make a stand. Do you have any ideas on that?"

In this field, Asana knew more than she did, and Ferla knew it. But he was still deferring to her.

"We'll know a good place when we see it," she said. "A cave with a narrow entrance would do. But there are none around here. At least so far."

"What about a steep slope?" Kubodin suggested.

Ferla did not much like the idea, but it was probably the best they could hope for.

"A steep slope would make it hard for hounds and for soldiers to attack us. But there would be nothing to stop them from taking their time and coming around at us from behind as well."

She had told them last night about the were-stones, and that the soldiers who pursued them might be transformed. All of them. It was a sickening feeling, knowing what might be done, what evil might be promulgated, in order to defeat them. Savanest was responsible for that, and if she could she would see that he faced a fitting punishment.

Ferla looked at her two friends. She had a plan, but she was not sure if they would like it.

"This is what I suggest," she said. "They *will* find us. There's nothing we can do about that. But we have time yet. Not much, but a little." She took a deep breath. "Instead of trying to find a place to defend, and we're not likely to find a good one, we can do this instead. Race hard to get well ahead of them. Then find a good spot where we can circle back, quite wide so they don't detect us, and then spring a trap on them from behind. If we catch them unprepared and downslope from us, especially with my bow, we can do a lot of damage to them before the hand-to-hand fighting begins."

They looked at her for a moment without answering. Asana looked grim, but once more not surprised. Kubodin whistled through his teeth though.

"You have guts, girl," he said.

23. The Storm Approaches

Ferla wasted no time. She set a fast pace, but it was one they could not keep up for long.

Yet they would not need to. When she found the right place, and then circled back to come up behind the enemy, they could rest then. When they struck, they would be fresh, while the enemy was tired from travel. So she hoped, anyway.

Whatever advantages she could obtain through all this were small, though. Would they be enough? She doubted it. But there was nothing left to do.

They moved ahead, three figures that scrabbled over the vast surface of Alithoras. The futility of life weighed down on her. What was it all for? Whether in a few hours, years or decades she would be dead. In a century, barely a memory of her would remain. If that. Nor would anything she did now, even if she succeeded in her aims, make a difference. The world, having forgotten her, would forget her deeds as well. Her existence would be blotted out just like the animals that dwelt in this land. How many generations of aurochs, or deer, or anything else had lived here? Where were they now, and who remembered them?

They were dust beneath her feet, she knew. And to dust she would turn one day too.

She gritted her teeth and strode ahead. Perhaps Savanest had done something to her. This was not the way she normally thought, and in truth, while she could not deny much of what she had considered, it was not quite right, either.

She had no wish to live forever. Aranloth had cured her of that. He was a man who had endured much, and time only made it worse, not better. But most of all, what she did now had a chance, slim though it was, of changing the world for the better. Her legacy would live long after her.

For if she did not stop Druilgar, she knew what would happen. Aranloth had told her much about the Morleth Stone, and like a sickness it would infect people. Evil would spread, and the darkness that had begun with the king, then spread to knights, the city and the realm, would spread all over the land.

Druilgar would be at its head, and he would bring war and death to neighboring lands, and seek to conquer all Alithoras if he could. The longer this went on, the stronger he would get and the harder to defeat.

It was up to her to stop that. Or at least to be the focal point for all those who would oppose it. That was her role, and that was the burden of the prophesy that had foretold her.

In the end, if she achieved that, she would have fulfilled her destiny. Nothing else mattered, and if she did die, at least she would die for a purpose worthy of such a sacrifice.

But it did gnaw at her that failure would not mean death. She understood now the opposing fate that evil had planned for her. That must never come to pass, and she vowed silently, in her heart, that she would force them to kill her rather than allow herself to be captured.

The afternoon passed, and they traveled with great haste, taking few breaks. Ever they looked behind them, studying the backtrail, but always they looked skyward too. Danger seemed to lie in wait all around them, but Ferla pushed that aside. She would do what she could, and it would work or it would not. There was nothing else to do, and fear, if she let it, would sap her of both strength and hope.

She would not let it.

The country began to change. It grew a little steeper, which was the kind of terrain that could be used to advantage. Also, rocks began to appear in the earth, often mostly their tips showing above the shorter grass, but sometimes they lay loose on the surface.

It was warm for a winter's day in the afternoon sun, which beat down from a clear sky, but it was also humid. In the east clouds gathered again, and another storm brewed.

They came at length to a steep slope. It was mostly grass, with just a few trees. But those trees grew thicker toward the top. The incline was the greatest one so far, and they pushed themselves to walk it. They were becoming tired now.

Kubodin led his mule up the slope, but the creature moved with surprising nimbleness, tackling both the steepness and the rough surface, littered with large rocks, easily.

The slope never seemed to end, but Ferla hoped it would provide them just the kind of place she was looking for to set a trap. But as they eventually neared the crest, the trees did indeed thicken into a band of forest. She feared if the forest continued down the other side that it would make a poor place to set an ambush. The trees would only provide cover to the enemy and the advantage of her bow would be lost. It was on the bow that her hopes rested to come out of this alive. But only if she could use it for a considerable amount of time before the enemy closed in to fighting range.

Kubodin stumbled and cursed, then righted himself and kept striding upward. He was tired now, as they all were.

Soon though, they at last reached the crest, which was almost flat, and entered the forest. It was dark here, and the humidity became stifling.

They walked ahead through the aisles of trees. It was strange here, for though the trees were stunted they were mostly pines, and there was still an ancient litter of needle-like leaves beneath their boots. The surface was new, but beneath that was the earthy remnants of leaves from centuries of windfalls.

Ferla moved with care. They could not see much, and walking was difficult. Because while the loamy soil was soft, often hard rocks lay beneath. Each step was different from the last, and only the mule seemed to move with ease. And perhaps Asana, who could make falling over appear graceful.

The level ground gave way swiftly, and Ferla's heart leaped. Before them fell away a steep slope, and the forest stopped abruptly, not marching down the incline but hugging only the crest of the ridge.

Better still, nothing grew on the slope. Not only were there no trees, but no grass either. It was a long, long incline of loose rocks.

They paused, looking down, and Ferla spoke. "This is it. This is what I've been looking for."

Asana and Kubodin studied the landscape with her. She knew what they were thinking, and how they were evaluating it. They were doing exactly as she had done.

"I agree," Asana said. "We'll not find a better place than this to set a trap."

Kubodin surveyed the land with his dark eyes, and then turned that gaze upon her.

"Nor can we travel much farther. Every hour like this saps us. Best to end this soon, and then rest. After the enemy comes up the slope that we just did to get here, they'll be tired. I know I am. That's the time to strike, especially once we're rested ourselves."

They hastened down the slope, and the stones were loose below them. They slipped and fell, and even Asana looked ill at ease. Only the mule negotiated it without mishap.

When they reached the bottom, Ferla looked back. Their trail was plain to see, and their scent would be there too. The enemy could not miss it, which was exactly what she wanted.

Before them, the land leveled out into a shallow basin. It looked like a dried lake, but it had been a long time since a body of water had lain here. It was a bowl of dust, and here too they left a trail that would be visible from above.

She took them to the other end of the dusty surface, but as soon as they were on grass again, she turned right.

"Time to hasten," she said. "If the enemy comes upon us before we're ready, all is lost."

Tired as they all were, they set a fast pace. At first, they kept going in the same direction, but eventually they swung back around and headed uphill again. This area was also covered by that same slippery surface of stones, though it was not as bad as where they had gone down. Ferla clambered up, and despite the fact that her thighs burned and she was constantly slipping on the loose surface, she shared a quick grin with Kubodin. She had wanted a good place for an ambush, and she had found one. If the enemy fell for the trap, they would be caught on this slope and her bow would be effective.

Eventually, they reached the top again. There, they had to rest, for they were breathing hard and bleeding from several falls. But they could not wait long. Not here. They had to get close enough to their original trail where they first descended the slope so that they could see the enemy when they arrived, but yet not so close that they could be detected themselves.

The forest was hushed around them as they walked, and they went ahead carefully because they could not know how close their pursuers were. But Ferla had been careful to angle around from the side that was downwind of where the enemy would be. They would not, at least she hoped, be scented by the were-hound.

"You have your bow," Kubodin said, "but some spears would serve us well also."

The little man took out his axe and wandered around the forest. From time to time the sound of his axe thudded through the quiet, and Ferla feared they would give themselves away to the enemy. Yet she did not think they were close enough to hear yet, and spears, even if they had no metal head, would give them another means of attack other than the bow.

Kubodin returned with a handful of saplings that he had cut down, all about the right thickness and six feet long. Then he went off to find some more.

"Let's get to work," Asana said.

They drew their knives and began to sharpen the end of the saplings. Somehow, Kubodin had managed to find hardwood. That was far better, for pine would be too light to do serious damage. Even the hardwood saplings would be useless against armor, but if any managed to strike exposed arms and legs, they would cause injuries. Injuries that might debilitate.

Kubodin returned with more, and they had about twenty all together. They were not likely to be able to use that many. They could not be thrown over anywhere near the distance that her bow could be used. By the time the enemy was in range, they would have closed the gap to about fifty feet.

She smiled grimly. Fifty paces up that slope was slow going. They might yet be able to use all those spears, and all the while there would be arrows flying too. The enemy would have a hard time of things indeed. If they fell for the trap.

The afternoon wore on, and they rested as best as they could. Ferla noticed that Kubodin had not tethered the mule, and indeed had removed its reins, saddle and carry bags where much of their dwindling supplies were kept. When the time arrived, it would be free to run.

She approved. They all knew what it meant, but none of them said anything. If they were to die here, then at least the mule could escape. She was glad of that.

As they waited, the storm built in the east, piling clouds on clouds until it looked ominous. This time, it was coming for them. Already the air felt strange, and a few gusts of wind picked up leaves and dust and blew them swirling through the air. No sooner did the leaves land than another gust lifted them, and from somewhere not that far away there was the dusty smell of new rain on the earth.

The wind picked up. It changed direction a few times, and Ferla feared it might swing the wrong way and take their scent to where the enemy was expected to show. If that happened, all was lost.

But the wind favored them, even if the rest of the weather did not. A pitter patter of rain came and went, and thunder rumbled. The towering storm drew closer, and it was much darker than it should be for this time of day, even though it was now late in the afternoon.

A hush fell over the forest. The only sound now was the wind in the tops of the trees, and the thunder. The three companions had positioned themselves behind a fallen tree trunk, itself victim likely enough to a storm such as the one that approached, but it must have been several years ago.

Lightning flashed, and even as it did the enemy appeared, following the trail that had been set for them. It was hard to see much, for it was hundreds of feet away, but Savanest was there, and he stood upon the ridge looking down the rocky slope. Yet he hesitated.

Perhaps he sensed the trap. Perhaps he was considering where best to find shelter against the storm, or if he should do so at all while his quarry might try to travel through it.

But for whatever reason, he hesitated. And he gave no signal for his followers to descend the slope.

24. Battle!

Savanest hesitated, and Ferla held her breath.

The servants of the once-knight milled behind him, and it was hard to see clearly because of the distance, trees and the dying light of the sun. Yet Ferla felt her heart skip a beat as she realized the men, every one of them, had now been transformed into were-beasts.

What evil could countenance such a thing? What man could inflict such an atrocity on fellow men?

Her hatred of Savanest flared to life. She knew that was wrong. She knew that such a strong emotion might jeopardize her judgement, but she could not help it.

She sensed Asana stiffen beside her, and Kubodin on her other side muttered unintelligibly under his breath.

The tension grew. Savanest remained poised on the ridge, but he did not descend. Lightning flared, splitting the sky, and thunder rumbled over the land. The storm was no longer distant, but drawing close, and the wind picked up, hurling debris through the forest and bending the tops of the trees.

Trying to be calm, Ferla strung her bow. It was a familiar action. It was ordinary, and by doing it she hoped to settle her mind. She must be rational and calculated here.

It did not work. She fumbled several times, and her heart continued to race. A cold sweat broke out on her forehead, and a spattering of rain lashed across her face. The wind blew it in sideways at her, but then the wind died away and in the momentary lull all seemed still and the rain stopped.

She waited, and in the temporary pause, where even nature held her breath, Savanest finally acted.

Slowly, the once-knight raised his hand, and then swiftly he brought it down. It was a signal, and all at once the were-beasts howled and grunted and barked. In a mad rush they leaped forward, and they tumbled in a chaotic group down the side of the slope in a frenzy. But for all their chaos, they were unified by the single purpose of pursuing the trail.

Savanest waited until they were all passed him, and then he too moved down the slope, going carefully. But for all his dignity, Ferla could not help feel that he was the one true beast of them all.

Ferla felt her heart pound. This was the moment she had planned for. She did not look at the other two. She knew they would be with her. Bounding up, she leaped over the fallen log and raced toward where the enemy had stood but moments ago.

It could still all go wrong. It could go terribly wrong. If she tarried too long, the enemy might be too far down the slope and away from them. If she were too quick, they might not be far enough down the slope and her opportunity to kill by arrow would be diminished.

Worst of all, Savanest could be cautious. He had time on his hands. He did not need to come back up the hill and attack. He would know such a move would cost him, and he might choose to stay right where he was until nightfall, and then climb the slope elsewhere and track her again.

They glided through the forest, and they left the mule behind. If any of them lived, they could come back for it.

The storm drew closer still, and lightning forked the sky. The trees danced around them, and a smattering of rain drove hard against their faces.

Ferla caught a glimpse of Asana. He was serene, and yet there was an alertness and determination about his face that forewarned trouble for the enemy. Not for the first time she was glad he was a friend. On her other side, Kubodin ran with his axe in his hand. There was a light of glee in his eyes, and the joy of battle was on him.

They passed through the forest like avenging wraiths. The wind tore at them, and lightning gleamed in their eyes and off their weapons.

Ferla slowed when she reached the point near where Savanest had stood. Crouching low, with the others nearby, she came to the very crest of the ridge and looked down.

The enemy was most of the way down the slope. She was neither too early nor too late. The were-beasts had spread out, trying to find a good path, but there was none. All about them the rocks turned and shifted under their tread, and it was worse now that rain had slickened them. She would not like to be caught down there and suffer attack by arrow. If that happened, she would seek cover. Yet now, she must incite the enemy to attack uphill.

Savanest was there too. He was among the beasts, though he was apart from them always. He commanded them by the power of the were-stones, but he was no comrade in arms. Perhaps that was to her advantage. He would not hesitate to see the beasts die. He might send them to attack where he would have spared a troop of men. Maybe.

Ferla stood, standing on the crest and no longer sheltered by trees. The wind tore at her clothes and slashed at her eyes. This much at least was not to her advantage. It would diminish the range of her bow and her accuracy.

She nocked an arrow, but then she hesitated. The enemy had not seen her, but could she loose an arrow into one of their backs?

A moment more she hesitated, and then she acted. This was war, and the enemy in her place would give her no quarter. She had no need to warn them, and yet she would. An arrow sped by surprise could scatter them and defeat her purposes. She needed them scrambling up the slope toward her instead.

She lowered her bow, and the wind fanned her red hair behind her.

"Hail, Savanest!" she shouted. "Coward knight and servant of the dark. Why do you run from me?"

Even above the rumble of thunder and the whistling of the wind along the stony slope, her voice carried.

Savanest spun around, drawing his sword. The were-beasts gathered around him, uncertain. Some howled and others grunted.

"You have come to me, girl." Savanest answered. He seemed not to shout at all, and yet his voice carried above the din of nature and beasts combined. It was in some way enhanced by magic. "I knew you would submit to my authority."

That sent a shiver of anger through Ferla's body, and yet she did not answer straightaway. To either side of her, Asana and Kubodin drove their spears into the ground point first. They could be grasped that way for throwing without wasting the time needed to bend to the ground and pick them up.

The anger that Ferla felt receded. In its place a wave of cold fear rolled over her. She remembered Savanest binding her when she spirit walked. She remembered the feeling of helplessness and acceptance of her fate like a deer with a wolf working its jaws into her throat. There was no point in resisting. Better to accept fate and let it run its course swiftly.

Then she understood. Savanest was not only using magic to enhance his voice, but also to strike at her as a weapon, to fill her mind with doubt and defeat.

She laughed, and she infused the sound with magic and drove it into the teeth of the wind. What skill did Savanest possess that she did not?

"Are you a knight, or a petty trickster, Savanest? You are not worthy to fight me. Flee! Begone, and take your ragtag band of slinking, servile beasts with you."

The were-beasts howled and barked and grunted at that. They understood her, and she knew they would.

Yet still she was surprised that her ploy worked.

In a frenzy, the beasts scrambled up the slope toward her. She had reached them, and insulted them. So too with Savanest, and if he had the power to recall his servants, the moment to do so had passed and was lost. He followed in the trail of the beasts.

Ferla marked a target. It was a hound, jaws slavering and eyes feral. It was, she thought, the one that had originally scented her trail. It had been a man, and somewhere within it the mind of that man still endured. She did not know if she did it a favor now, or if it wanted to live. But if *she* were to live, or evade a fate even worse than the hound's, she must kill it and as many of the others as she could take.

She released her breath slowly, and her first arrow winged through the wind. It was a distant target, and conditions were bad with both the wind and the slope to contend with. Yet still the arrow flew true, and even as the hound stumbled over a rock that turned beneath the weight of its paws, the arrow hit it square in the chest.

The hound leaped in the air and howled. When it fell, the arrow was buried deep in it, and it worried it with its massive jaws.

Blood frothed on those jaws, and darkened the thick fur of its chest. But it clambered no more up the slope, and Ferla ignored it.

This was but the beginning of a battle that would decide her fate, and that of her companions whom she loved.

25. Through Their Eyes

Ferla did not hasten. She trusted her skill with the bow, and her long years of practice.

To her, she was not moving fast, yet to the others it would seem so. Her movements were slick and smooth, and another arrow was nocked and the bow drawn in little more than a heartbeat.

Against her nose and cheek, she felt the bow string. For a moment, she hesitated. Savanest was her main target, but she had no clear line of sight. If she killed him, it was possible that the magic of the were-stone that was used to control the beasts would be directionless, and they would scatter. It seemed unlikely, but it was worth the attempt.

Savanest stumbled over a rock, and she released her breath letting the arrow speed away. Even as she drew another one from her quiver, she watched the speeding arrow through the air.

But the knight had guessed she would attempt this, and even as he stumbled he righted himself and moved behind a beast again. Her arrow struck the beast, but it was not a killing blow. It yelped, but came on with the arrow sticking out of its flank.

Ferla wasted no more time on Savanest. She marked the closest beast scrambling up the slope. It was a thing on four legs, still part human, covered in bristling hide and with the tusks of a boar protruding from its face.

The arrow flew true, taking the beast in the throat. It reared up, and when it screamed the voice was human. But it fell to the ground, and those who were once its comrades in arms but now its packmates scrambled over it as they climbed the slope.

Another arrow sung through the air. It took a beast in the eye, and it tumbled backward to trip and cast over those who came directly behind.

And so it went. Ferla had no sense of time. All that existed in the entire universe was that rocky slope, the beasts and the plying of her deadly skill. All over the slope the evidence of that skill lay in tumbled heaps. They were dead, or dying. Blood soaked the rocks, and screams rent the air louder than the thunder.

She heard little of it. She saw little of it. There was only nock, pull, aim and release. And ever she aimed for those beasts that led the chaotic charge against her. Each time that one fell the others jostled around it, seeking to avoid its flailing claws or gnashing teeth. Unless they were bigger, in which case they trampled over it uncaring in their lust to reach her. But each death bought her a moment of extra time to loose another arrow.

Until there were no more arrows. She reached back to her quiver and grasped empty air. Her stock was used up, yet still the beasts were coming, and they were close now.

Ferla cast aside the bow, now useless, and drew her sword. For the first time she looked upon the death she had wrought, and saw that the slope was littered with bodies. Yet still more than twenty beasts came on, and behind them was Savanest, still using them as protection.

Nearby, Kubodin yelled a wild battle cry, and he pulled a spear from the ground and cast it into the onrushing attackers.

On her other side, Asana did the same, only silently. But the spears were not steel tipped, and the beasts large. Some of the enemy fell, and some were wounded, but most came on despite the rain of sharpened shafts.

Ferla could see their eyes now. The drip of saliva frothing at their snouts or the glint of rain on tusks. She heard their baying and grunting, and once more fear surged over her. The enemy were too many, and there was no way to fight such beasts, and still there remained the knight himself, more deadly still.

And she cursed that she had spent all her arrows, for now she had a clear view of him, but no means to kill him.

She thought of attacking with magic, but it was not her best skill and she must keep that in reserve to counter anything the knight himself might do.

The last of the spears was thrown, and then bright blades flashed. The three companions drew close so that they might protect each other and prevent themselves from being surrounded.

A beast with the body of a hound and the head of a boar tried to gut Asana with massive tusks, but his blade whipped out slicing down the side of the creature's neck and sending arterial blood spurting high into the air.

Yet still he was knocked back by the weight of the dying beast. Kubodin cried out, and his axe swung in a glittering arc and it severed the leg of a hound that leaped toward his friend.

Ferla faced her own enemy. A beast shambled toward her, rising on two legs like a bear. It roared in her face, saliva flying and lightning flaring behind it to make it seem otherworldly. Her sword gutted it, but still the great claws came down and smashed against her side sending her flying.

If not for the armor, she might have died. Yet she feared some of her ribs were broken. She rose and leaped back toward her friends. They must not be separated otherwise the enemy would surround them and pull them down one by one.

The bear creature came at her again, shuffling forward on two legs but trampling its own intestines. Rage drove it, and magic drove that rage. She hacked at it again, half severing its head and avoiding another smashing claw. But even as she did so a were-beast like a wolf, smaller than the others but nimble, leaped at her throat.

The creature smashed into her, bearing her back, and she felt its hot breath on her neck. She turned and stepped back, flinging it from her and bringing her sword up in a slashing movement.

The wolf thing howled, blood flowing from the bottom of its snout, and tried to close again.

Ferla moved into Tempest Blows the Dust, her sword arcing up and down. Several times she struck the beast, and it fell away. She had not forgotten the bear, but Kubodin had cracked his axe against the massive head and it had finally fallen to the ground like a logged tree.

She knew what was happening then, and it sickened her. The creatures had not tried to kill her. They had tried to bring her down to the ground. From there, she could be captured.

Better to die than that, but she had no more time for thought. Another were-hound came at her, lips parted in a rictus growl, teeth showing and eyes fixed in hatred. She fended it off, but she saw Asana stumble.

Dead creatures lay around the sword master, but blood welled from a bite in his arm, and it was his sword arm too. Yet somehow he managed to take the hilt of the blade in his left hand, and he fought nearly as well that way as with his right.

The three companions were being overwhelmed though, and Ferla felt the maddening frustration of that. There was nothing to do but fall back, which they did. But the advantage of the slope that had served them so well was lost now.

They fought within the first few trees of the forest, but they could use no trunk to guard their rear. Instead, they formed a tight circle, fighting back to back. But if one fell, then the other two would be exposed to attack from two sides at once.

Kubodin cried out some war cry that she had never heard before. His great axe, Discord, flashed in deadly arcs. Asana fought silently, barely seeming to move but evading attacks and dealing death with sublime grace. Ferla herself, though her arm was beyond tired and her breath heaved in her chest like fire, fought off her own attackers.

It could not go on. The were-beasts were frenzied, and though most of them had fallen since that first arrow, there were still enough left to overwhelm tiring opponents. And behind them all, she caught glimpses of Savanest, not risking himself in the battle but ready to pounce when he could and take her prisoner.

"I will never be a Morleth Knight!" she screamed, and from some hidden depth new strength flowed into her. She laid about her with her sword, dealing death. The beasts withdrew from her, dismayed.

But her new strength did not last long. It was the last ebb of her defiance, and she stumbled.

The enemy were on her again. Jaws snapping, howls rending the air. Even as a great were-hound leaped at her, silhouetted by a streak of lightning that sizzled through the air nearby, she tripped and the beast smashed into her chest.

The earth shook with thunder even as she crashed to the ground, the weight of the beast atop her. Somehow, she lost a grip of her sword, and her two hands came up to grab the creature's neck, trying to throw it off her.

It was to no avail. It was too heavy and too strong for her. Had it wanted to kill her, it could have. Its fetid breath was hot against her exposed neck, but it did not try to bite

Another hound joined the first, and the weight was crushing. Her only hope was help from either Asana or Kubodin, but that did not come. She could not see them, and they may even be dying themselves as she lay there. Or perhaps they could not reach her.

Her hands gripped the thick fur, and she strained with all her might to shift the creature off her, but she was not strong enough, and knew it.

Yet she did not give up. She would never give up, and as she heaved the pale were-stone glimmered before her eyes against the dark hair of the beast. How she hated it!

She could sense the evil of the thing. It infuriated her. What mind could encompass the making of such a thing? What mind could invoke its magic?

Savanest had done so though, and it occurred to her that she could also. What he could do, she could as well. But dare she?

She would never do so. Not for the purposes Savanest had. But to save her life? To save herself from capture and being brought before the Morleth Stone? Some instinct flared to life that transcended morals. It surged through her, giving her hope, however desperate.

Her hand crept through the fur. Suddenly her fingers touched the stone, and then she gripped it in a fist. It was cold against her skin, but she felt the magic of it and her own sparked to life.

The two magics met, and she pulsed her power into the depths of the cold stone. Suddenly she was one with the were-beasts. She sensed what they sensed and felt what they felt. She sensed their animal natures, but so too what remained of them that was human. She saw through their eyes, and perceived also the overriding command sent by

Savanest himself, for he too was connected by magic to all the stones.

Even as she became aware of him, he became aware of her. She felt his shock though that she had touched the stones and joined her magic to them. That was to her advantage and she acted swiftly to use it before he thought to counter her.

She hated what she was doing, but swiftly she sent an image to the beasts of them rending each other. She sent the thought to them that they must kill one another, for they were their own true enemies.

The were-beasts yelped and howled. The two atop her began to fight, and she feared they would kill her by accident as they snarled and bit each other. But she held firm to the were-stone, and the chain that secured it to the beast snapped as it rolled off her.

Snatching up her sword in her left hand she sprang to her feet. Blood dripped from her right hand where the chain had ripped into her flesh.

She ignored the pain. Looking around, she saw Asana and Kubodin were still up. They were drawing closer to her and away from the beasts that fought each other. They wanted no part of that battle.

Through the stone in her hand, she felt Savanest try to wrench control of the beasts back from her. She defied it with all her will, but she knew instinctively she was at a disadvantage. The stone she held was connected by magic to all the rest, but it was not the controlling stone.

The fight she now fought was every bit as fierce as the one she was fighting just before. But this was invisible, and a contest of will alone. She held in her mind the image of the beasts attacking one another. But she saw also Savanest's image of them turning and rending the flesh of Asana and Kubodin.

Ferla went down on one knee with the strain of the battle. Through the stone she sensed Savanest's triumph, and it was at just that moment that she decided to attack him.

She dropped the sword and from her left hand lòhren-fire darted toward the knight, and he leaped out of the way in surprise. But his concentration was broken, and she wrested control of the beasts fully to herself.

She sensed the fighting that was going on, felt jaws on throats crushing away life, saw in her mind claws ripping open bellies. She was aware of it all and the slipping away into death of those she was connected to.

Asana and Kubodin must have had some glimmer of recognition of what was going on. They sped toward Savanest to distract him from his battle with her. She sensed Savanest's dark sorcery rise and almost felt the heat of it as he scattered fire at them.

The two men dodged, but still some of the blast hit them and they were sent sprawling. But Ferla kept her will on the beasts and the last two of them died, killing each other.

Her anger flared anew then. She had been forced into using the dark sorcery of the stone, and she knew she would use it yet once more.

She strode toward Savanest, and warned her two friends.

"Stay back," she ordered. "I have this now. Savanest is mine."

"Nay," the knight answered. "You are *mine*."

She knew what he would attempt, and was ready for it. Indeed, she was already doing it herself to him. Through the were-stone she sent a pulse of magic and invoked its own dark sorcery. She would transform Savanest into a beast as he had done to his men. No punishment could be more fitting.

Her magic and his clashed. Her will fought against his. The dark sorcery of the stone built up, towering invisibly and ready to unleash itself. But neither Morleth Knight nor Kingshield Knight, for so she knew she now was, held the ascendancy.

The storm raged around them, with lashing rain and wind. Hail fell, smashing into the stones of the slope and hammering into the boughs of the trees, bringing down leaves.

Ferla ignored it. It was nothing compared to the battle being fought.

Asana and Kubodin were ready to attack, but they held their positions. They trusted her, and followed her order. But if she faltered they would launch themselves at the knight. And surely die.

So she stepped closer, and redoubled her efforts to drive the sorcery of the were-stone into Savanest.

The knight attacked her. Not with magic or steel, but with words.

"Fool girl! Join us, and the world will be yours. Defy us, and even if you live all your friends will perish. Especially Faran, for we have learned where he goes and already a trap is set for him."

Ferla felt her emotions reeling. She could not bear to lose Faran. Not ever. But was this merely an attempt to distract her?

Her will faltered, and Savanest stepped toward her with confidence.

"Join me, and I will save Faran. Defy me, and he will die."

It was too much to bear. How could she make such a choice? But she knew what Faran would want. And over and above his life, and hers, she had a responsibility. Faladir needed her. Her people needed her.

She gathered her will, and drove it with her anger. "We would both rather die. I am the seventh knight, and I judge you and sentence you."

Even as she spoke she hurled her magic into the stone. Savanest reeled back, and she strode toward him. She was no longer Ferla. She was the seventh knight of legend and prophesy, and her rage was terrible.

Tears streamed down her face, for she may have condemned Faran, but she stood above her adversary and unleashed the power of the were-stone.

Savanest tried to resist, but she overwhelmed him. The knight screamed, and held up a hand imploringly. She ignored the gesture.

The magic roared through him, and he screamed again. Hair sprouted all over him, and became fur. He lifted high his head, and Ferla heard bones crack and lengthen. His body changed, and muscles swelled until his clothes split. He bent and gnawed with great teeth at belt and boots, worrying at them until they came free.

Savanest, once a Kingshield Knight was become a beast, and Ferla was glad. He had got what he deserved. Had she been merciful, she would have killed him. Instead, she flung out an arm.

"Flee!" she commanded. "Run, and haunt the wild as an animal. Shun men, but know that once you were one!"

The beast stood trembling, a deep growl throbbing in its throat, and then the force of the magic that controlled it took full force. It leaped away into the forest and was gone.

Asana gazed at her, his clothes torn and bloodied, his eyes full of sympathy, and perhaps even shock at her sense of justice. But he did not disagree, else he would have spoken.

Kubodin merely grinned at her. "Now that's what I call fitting," he said.

The storm faded. They found shelter from the remnants of it in the forest, and tended their wounds. They were lucky to be alive, and knew it. Asana had fared worst, being bitten and raked by claws. He would need days of rest to recover, but that would not happen. They could not stay here, but must continue to flee or risk being found again.

Yet that was not her greatest concern.

Epilogue

When their wounds were bandaged and they had rested briefly, Ferla insisted they find the bodies of each of the beasts. She would not risk the were-stones ever being found and used again.

It was a grim task, but they each carried it out without complaint. No one disagreed that it was necessary.

Destroying the stones was a harder matter, though. Night had set around them by the time they were done, and for once they lit a fire. Cold, wet and wounded they had need of warmth. And Ferla surmised it would be the only way to destroy the stones.

She did not think they were indestructible as the Morleth Stone was. But the task would require heat. Heat, and magic.

When they had rested as long as they dared, she cast the stones into the fire and then fed it with her magic until it leaped as high as the treetops in twining columns of multihued brilliance that tore the night. The others, holding her up for she nearly fell, were solemn.

When she was done, she withdrew her magic and the fire winked out. Only a black hollow in the ground was left, full of greasy ashes. Kubodin, holding a flaming branch, kicked it with his boots, searching for any remnant of the stones.

"Gone," he said. "And good riddance."

"Time for us to be gone also," Ferla told them.

She could barely stand and they knew it. But they did not argue. They would not spend the night here with the corpses of the beasts all around, and the threat of being found.

"But where do we go to?" Asana asked, and there was sympathy in his eyes as there always seemed to be when he looked at her.

Ferla was not sure of the answer. It was an impossible choice.

Was it possible Savanest had tricked her? Were his words mere deceit intended to distract during battle?

She did not believe so. The magic had connected them, and at that moment she would have sensed any lie. A part of her was in his mind.

No. Faran was found. And he would die. Unless, perhaps, she could reach him in time. But that would mean putting aside her duty as seventh knight. Could she choose between love and duty?

She moved off into the night without giving answer. The storm had cleared and the air was fresh. The sweet scent of wet grass, pine and damp herbage came to her. The world was beautiful, but just now it meant nothing to her.

Asana, and Kubodin, having since retrieved his mule, followed silently. She did not tell them her final choice. Nor did they ask.

Thus ends *The Sworn Knight.* The Kingshield series continues in book five, *The Scarlet Knight.* Therein, Faran will discover more of his true destiny. And where the evil of the Morleth Stone will bend its dark will to destroying him. For it cannot allow him to live…

THE SCARLET KNIGHT

BOOK FIVE OF THE KINGSHIELD SERIES

COMING SOON

Dedication

There's a growing movement in fantasy literature. Its name is noblebright, and it's the opposite of grimdark.

Noblebright celebrates the virtues of heroism. It's an old-fashioned thing, as old as the first story ever told around a smoky campfire beneath ancient stars. It's storytelling that highlights courage and loyalty and hope for the spirit of humanity. It recognizes the dark, the dark in us all, and the dark in the villains of its stories. It recognizes death, and treachery and betrayal. But it dwells on none of these things.

I dedicate this book, such as it is, to that which is noblebright. And I thank the authors before me who held the torch high so that I could see the path: J.R.R. Tolkien, C.S. Lewis, Terry Brooks, David Eddings, Susan Cooper, Roger Taylor and many others. I salute you.

And, for a time, I too shall hold the torch high.

Appendix: Encyclopedic Glossary

Note: the glossary of each book in this series is individualized for that book alone. Additionally, there is often historical material provided in its entries for people, artifacts and events that are not included in the main text.

Many races dwell in Alithoras. All have their own language, and though sometimes related to one another the changes sparked by migration, isolation and various influences often render these tongues unintelligible to each other.

The ascendancy of Halathrin culture, combined with their widespread efforts to secure and maintain allies against elug incursions, has made their language the primary means of communication between diverse peoples.

This glossary contains a range of names and terms. Many are of Halathrin origin, and their meaning is provided. The remainder derive from native tongues and are obscure, so meanings are only given intermittently.

Often, names of Camar and Halathrin elements are combined. This is especially so for the aristocracy. Few other tribes had such long-term friendship with the immortal Halathrin as the Camar, and though in this relationship they lost some of their natural culture, they gained nobility and knowledge in return.

List of abbreviations:

Cam. Camar

Comb. Combined

Cor. Corrupted form

Chg: Cheng

Hal. Halathrin

Leth. Letharn

Prn. Pronounced

Agrak: A rune of several strokes radiating from a central point. It represents a group of doves taking flight from the ground and signifies the word "flee".

Alithoras: *Hal.* "Silver land." The Halathrin name for the continent they settled after leaving their own homeland. Refers to the extensive river and lake systems they found and their wonder at the beauty of the land.

Aranloth: *Hal.* "Noble might." A lòhren of ancient heritage. Travels Alithoras under different names and guises.

Asana: *Chg.* "Gift of light." Rumored to be the greatest sword master in the history of the Cheng people. His father was a Duthenor tribesman.

Bouncing Stone (the): An ancient inn built at the same time as the Tower of the Stone. It is said a smithy occupied the land previously, and here of old attempts were made to destroy the Morleth Stone.

Brand: *Duth.* A heroic figure in Alithoras. Both warrior and lòhren. Stories of his exploits have spread over the land, and they kindle hope wherever they are heard.

Caludreth: *Cam.* "Lord of the waves." A poetic term in Camar literature for a ship. Once a Kingshield Knight.

Cardoroth: *Cor. Hal. Comb. Cam.* A Camar city, often called Red Cardoroth. Some say this alludes to the red granite commonly used in the construction of its buildings, others that it refers to a prophecy of destruction. If so, Brand appears to have thwarted it.

Cheng: *Chg.* "Warrior." The overall name of the various related tribes that dwell in the northwest of Alithoras. It was a word for warrior in the dialect of a tribe that rose to supremacy and set an emperor above all the various clans to unite them.

Conduil: *Cam.* Etymology obscure. The first king of Faladir. He broke the Siege of Faladir and founded the order of Kingshield Knights, of which he was the first.

Danath Elbar: *Hal.* "Underground mansion." Halls delved by the Halathrin into the stone of Nuril Faranar, the mountain used at times as a command post during the Shadowed Wars.

Death-sleep: A state of suspended animation used by lòhrens of the highest order to heal from terrible wounds. It also prolongs life, for it allows the body to repair itself. It requires great skill and magic, but the practice is not without extreme risks. Especially to the mind.

Discord: The name of Kubodin's axe. It has two blades. One named Chaos and the other Spite.

Dromdruin: *Cam.* "Valley of the ancient woods." One of many valleys in the realm of Faladir. Home of Faran, and birthplace throughout the history of the realm of many Kingshield Knights.

Drùgluck: A pattern of three slanted lines, going from right to left and each one longer than the previous. Used by some creatures of the shadow as a warning to stay away from a place because it is a sacred area that serves as a gateway between the spirit and normal worlds. Such areas are used in ceremonies and invocations for help or retribution against enemies. It is believed that at certain cycles of the moon and seasons the barriers that separate the worlds are weakened and the gateway opens. Also marks a place where the effects of sorcery linger or where there is some unspecified but lethal danger. Often it signifies several of these things at once.

Druilgar: *Hal.* "Spear star – a comet." King of Faladir, and First Knight of the Kingshield Knights. Descendent of King Conduil.

Duthenor: *Duth.* "The people." A tribe of people farther to the west of Camar lands. Related to the Camar, and sharing many common legends and experiences. But different also.

Elves: See Halathrin.

Elù-drak: *Hal.* "Shadow wings." A creature of the dark. Deadly, and used by sorcerers to gather information and assassinate chosen victims. The female of the species is the most dangerous, having the power to inspire terror and bend victims to her will. Few can resist. Of old, even great warriors succumbed and willingly let the creature take their life. One of the more terrible creatures of the Old World.

Elùgai: *Hal. Prn.* Eloo-guy. "Shadowed force." The sorcery of an elùgroth.

Elù-haraken: *Hal.* "Shadowed wars." Long ago battles in a time that is become myth to the scattered Camar tribes.

Faladir: *Cam.* "Fortress of Light." A Camar city founded out of the ruinous days of the elù-haraken.

Faran: *Cam.* "Spear of the night – a star." A name of good luck. Related to the name Dardenath, though of a later layer of linguistic change. A young hunter from Dromdruin valley. His grandfather was a Kingshield Knight, though not the first of their ancestors to be so.

Ferla: *Cam.* "Unforeseen bounty." A young hunter from Dromdruin valley.

First Knight: The designated leader of the Kingshield Knights.

Halathrin: *Hal.* "People of Halath." A race of elves named after an honored lord who led an exodus of his people to the land of Alithoras in pursuit of justice, having sworn to defeat a great evil. They are human, though of fairer form, greater skill and higher culture. They possess a unity of body, mind and spirit that enables insight and endurance beyond the native races of Alithoras. Said to be immortal, but killed in great numbers during their conflicts in ancient times with the evil they sought to destroy. Those conflicts are collectively known as the Shadowed Wars.

Harakgar (the): *Leth.* "The three sisters." Creatures of magic brought into being by the Letharn. Their purpose is to protect the tombs of their creators from robbery.

Hundred (the): A resistance group established in Faladir to prepare the way for the coming of the seventh knight.

Kareste: *Hal.* "Ice unlocking – the spring thaw." A lòhren of mysterious origin. Friend to Aranloth, but usually more active farther north in Alithoras than Faladir.

Kingshield Knights: An order of knights founded by King Conduil. Their sacred task is to guard the indestructible Morleth Stone from theft and use by the evil forces of the world. They are more than great warriors, being trained in philosophy and the arts also. In addition to their prime function as guards, they travel the land at whiles dispensing justice and offering of their wisdom and council.

Kubodin: *Chg.* Etymology unknown. A wild hillman from the lands of the Cheng. Simple appearing, but far more than he seems. Asana's manservant.

Lady of the Land (the): The spirit of the land. It is she whom lòhrens serve, though her existence is seldom discussed.

Letharn: *Hal.* "Stone raisers. Builders." A race of people that in antiquity conquered most of Alithoras. Now, only faint traces of their civilization endure.

Lindercroft: *Cam.* “Rising mountain crashes – a wave rolling into the seashore.” A Kingshield Knight. Youngest of the order.

Lòhren: *Hal. Prn.* Ler-ren. “Knowledge giver – a counselor.” Other terms used by various nations include wizard, druid and sage.

Lòhren-fire: A defensive manifestation of lòhrengai. The color of the flame varies according to the skill and temperament of the lòhren.

Magic: Mystic power. See lòhrengai and elùgai.

Maldurn: *Cam.* “Swimming eel.” A soldier of Faladir. His name is typical of some inland villages of the realm where the tradition of ocean related names is maintained but adapted to the local environment.

Menendil: *Hal.* “Sign of hope.” Sometimes called Mender. His is an old family, and he can trace his lineage back to the days before the founding of Faladir to a liegeman of the then chieftain. Unusually, his name is not of Camar origin. Family history records that his forefather was a seer, and was greatly esteemed by his lord.

Morleth Stone: *Hal.* “Round stone.” The name signifies that such a stone is not natural. It is formed by elùgai for sorcerous purposes. The stone is strengthened by arcane power to act as a receptacle of enormous force. Little is known of their making and uses except that they are rare and that elùgroths perish during their construction. The stone guarded by the Kingshield Knights in Faladir is said to be the most powerful of all that were created. And to be sentient.

Norgril: *Cam.* "Leaping fish." A member of the Hundred.

Norla: *Cam.* "Fish hunter – fisherman." Wife of Menendil.

Nuatha: *Cam.* "Silver wanderer – a stream." A vagabond healer that travels widely throughout Faladir. Aranloth in one of his guises.

Nuril Faranar: *Hal.* "Lonely watchman." A single mountain rising above the flat lands that border Halathar. Used as a vantage point and command post for several great battles during the elù-haraken. Currently under the guardianship of Asana. For this, Aranloth interceded on his behalf.

Nurthil Wood: *Cam.* "Dark secrets." A great forest north of Faladir. Home to outlaws and disaffected from the wide lands all around. Once, a stronghold of the forces of darkness, but cleansed by succeeding kings of Faladir.

Osahka: *Leth.* "The guide – specifically a spiritual or moral guide." A title of enormous reverence and respect. Applied to Aranloth for his role as spiritual leader of the Kingshield Knights.

Savanest: *Cam.* "Subtle skill." A Kingshield Knight. All the knights think of each other as brothers. But Savanest and Sofanil are also brothers by blood.

Shadow Fliers: See elù-drak.

Shadowed Lord (the): Once, a lòhren. But he succumbed to evil and pursued forbidden knowledge and powers. He created an empire of darkness and struck to conquer all Alithoras during the elù-haraken. He was defeated, but his magic had become greater than any ever known. Some say he will return from death to finish the war he started. Whether that is so, no one knows. But the order of lòhrens guard against it, and many evils that served him yet live.

Shadowed Wars: See elù-haraken.

Sofanil: *Cam.* "Sharp of wits." A Kingshield Knight. All the knights think of each other as brothers. But Sofanil and Savanest are also brothers by blood.

Sorcerer: See elùgroth.

Sorcery: See elùgai.

Three Sisters: See harakgar.

Tower of the Stone: The tower King Conduil caused to be built to serve as the guarding structure of the Morleth Stone. Some claim his sarcophagus rests upon its pinnacle, as it was the custom of some ancient Camar royalty to be interred on a high place where the lights of the sun, moon and stars still lit their long sleep.

Way of the Sword: The martial aspect of the training of a Kingshield Knight.

Were-beast: A creature of the shadow. Said to be able to shapeshift from animal to human form.

Were-hound: A creature of the shadow that takes the form of a dog.

Were-stone: An artifact of sorcery. Used by elùgroths in ancient days to control servants and transform them against their will into beasts. Different stones have slightly different powers, and thus different beasts are created. Usually formed out of pearls, but not always.

Wizard: See lòhren.

About the author

I'm a man born in the wrong era. My heart yearns for faraway places and even further afield times. Tolkien had me at the beginning of *The Hobbit* when he said, ". . . one morning long ago in the quiet of the world . . ."

Sometimes I imagine myself in a Viking mead-hall. The long winter night presses in, but the shimmering embers of a log in the hearth hold back both cold and dark. The chieftain calls for a story, and I take a sip from my drinking horn and stand up . . .

Or maybe the desert stars shine bright and clear, obscured occasionally by wisps of smoke from burning camel dung. A dry gust of wind marches sand grains across our lonely campsite, and the wayfarers about me stir restlessly. I sip cool water and begin to speak.

I'm a storyteller. A man to paint a picture by the slow music of words. I like to bring faraway places and times to life, to make hearts yearn for something they can never have, unless for a passing moment.

Printed in Great Britain
by Amazon

60134742R00121